IT'S ALL COMING BACK TO ME NOW

The secret

BY LOVELY WHITMORE

ISBN 978-1479264438

John, you have been my biggest supporter and best friend. Thank you.

Randy Jackson turned the Lexus onto Honey Grove Circle. He couldn't help but wonder how things would go from this point on. Would Latrease talk to him, or would she continue to be as silent as she had been during the drive home from the hospital? He knew they would have to talk, he just didn't know when it would happen. Would she yell at him and cast him out of her life, or would she be understanding? His mind continued to ramble on the conversation they had had in the Walmart parking lot, only twenty minutes earlier. Latrease had said she wanted to leave. She didn't want anything to do with him. He was clueless as to what it was going to take get her to change her mind, and stay with him.

Why would she, he wondered. Why would anyone want to stay with a man that had lied the way he did? Why would any woman want to raise her child with a man that did what he did? He kept telling himself that he had done the right thing, but why did it feel so wrong? Why did it feel so cruel?

He parked the car in the garage and walked over to assist Latrease with the baby. She had detached the car seat from the base. She smiled at the sleeping infant. "She is so adorable, Randy." She handed him the carrier after realising it was a bit too heavy to lift.

"Yes I know."

Randy grabbed the diaper bag that lay on the back seat. Latrease closed the door. He followed as she walked up the steps to the front door of the guesthouse. She unlocked the door and opened it.

"SURPRISE!"

Randy was startled. He hadn't told anyone but his mother that Latrease was coming home from the hospital that day. She had assured him that she would not bother her until Latrease had a few days to rest.

"Mom, what is this?" Randy put the carrier on the sofa and gave a hard stare in his mother's direction.

Latrease put her purse on the end table. Bernard, Bertha, Shemeka and the twins were standing in the living room. They were all smiling about something, but Randy wasn't sure what it was.

"We have a surprise for Latrease." Randys' mother walked over to the bedroom, opened the door, and waved her hand.

"I'm so tired, Ms Scott, can we do this another time?" Latrease walked over in front of the couch where the baby was and slid down on the seat with one leg folded under her bottom.

"I don't think so, it's been long enough." Randys' mom said in a matter of fact way.

"Come on in darling." Ms Scott motioned for the person in the bedroom to come into the living room.

A woman that looked identical to Latrease, stepped into the dining room.
"Hi sis." The woman waved. Latrease jumped like she had seen a ghost.

"Oh my goodness! Latrease, are you alright?" Randy rushed to her side and grabbed her hand in his.

"She'll be fine, she's just excited to see me, aren't you sis?"

"What are you doing here?" Latrease murmured.

"Wow! Is that how you greet your twin sister that you haven't seen in almost two years?" the lady put her hand on her hip.

"I'm sorry; I'm just surprised to see you." Latrease wrapped her arms around the woman.

"Yeah, I see. You've gained a few pounds since the last time I saw you."

"I just had a baby, Shanice, what did you expect?"

"Yeah, I heard about that, it's kinda messed up that I'm just now finding out about all this, where's the baby daddy?"

"That would be me." Randy stood up reached his hand out to shake the hand of the woman that looked identical to Latrease.

"Wait a minute, what did you just say, Randy?" Randy watched his mom put her hand on her hip.

"All these months you been running around here telling us Latrease was your patient, why in the world would you…"

"It's a long story mom…" Randy took a deep breath. He knew this was neither the time nor place to talk about this; but then again he was just glad to get it out.

"Latrease, how could you lie to us like that? After all we have done for you." Bertha snapped rolling her eyes.

"I never meant to…"

"It was not her fault, she didn't remember." Randy cut her off.

"I thought my life was complicated," Shanice chucked, "But you, sis, you have *me* beat."

Randy watched the girls hug. Shemeka walked over to the dining room table, pulled a chair out and sat down.

"Latrease how come you never told us you had a twin sister?" Kevin blurted out.

"I didn't remember."

"You mean to tell me you forgot about me?"

"Niecy, it's complicated. I'm so tired right now. How did you find me?"

"Umm, actually, I found her!" Shemeka exclaimed.

"Eh hmm" Kevin cleared his throat. "I saw her first auntie."

Latrease sat down on the couch next to the carrier that the baby was lying in. She picked up the pacifier that had fallen into the carrier and handed it to Randy.

"Can you rinse that off for me?" Randy nodded, grabbed the pacifier and walked into the kitchen. Bernard followed him.

"What's going on bruh?" Bernard crossed his chest with his arms.

"It's complicated man."

"I understand that, but man…I thought we were closer that."

Randy looked in his brothers eyes. "I couldn't tell you, I couldn't risk her finding out."

"That doesn't make sense Randy."

"Her condition, look, she had a rare type of amnesia. She had to remember on her own. You would have told Bertha and that blabbermouth would have told her. I couldn't take the risk."

"If you would have told me something as serious as this, what makes you think I would have told Bertha?" Bernard raised his brows.

"You know you would have, you can't hold water."

"Yeah, well it's still messed up man."

Calvin and Kevin, walked into the kitchen. "Hey Unk, how come you never told us Latrease was a twin too?"

"I never knew myself. *This* is new to me."

"No wonder she never asked us any of those questions that most people ask twins; like if we can feel each others pain and stuff." Calvin said looking at his brother.

"Yeah and she always knew us apart too." Kevin added.

"How did you guys find her?" Randy asked while he turned the handle on the facet.

"Auntie Shemeka, took us to get our drivers license today. While we were in the waiting room, we saw Shanice leaving out of the other room. She looked dead at us and kept walking."

"Then I called out to her. I was like Latrease what are you doing here; ain't you 'spose to be in the hospital still?"

"She looked at us and then laughed." Kevin grabbed the pacifier from Randy, "I'll take this to her." He said and left the kitchen.

"Then what happened?" Randy asked Calvin.

"She said 'you must have me mistaken for someone else.' Then she walked out of the building".

"Auntie Shemeka was coming in as she was walking out. Then they started talking outside and the next thing I knew they were both coming inside. Auntie Shemeka said that Shanice was Latrease's twin sister and she was going to take her to the hospital to see Latrease. She got on the phone and called grandma and then she said we would just come here because y'all were already on the way home. Latrease don't seem to be too happy to see her though."

Randy glanced at his brother, who was now shaking his head. "I still can't believe you left me in the dark all these months like that Randy."

"Unk, how did Latrease remember anyway?"

"I guess when she saw her."

"No. I'm talking about you and her and Keyana."

"I don't know. We were in the car this morning on the way here and she just started going off on me. I really don't know what triggered…"

The door to the kitchen swung open.

"Randy, how could you keep this from us?" Ms Scott walked over and poked her finger into his chest.

"I have a granddaughter and you weren't gonna tell me she was yours."

"I'm sorry mom, I had to do what I had to do. You know this was hard on me. I've never had to keep something so serious from you. I feel bad but I had a good reason."

Ms Scott sighed. "Well it really hurts my feelings that you didn't tell me. I'mma get up to the house and start dinner. We need to give this child some time to talk to her sister alone. Bernard, y'all come over for dinner tonight, ok."

"*A*re you alright?" Latrease Wilson felt someone tapping on her shoulder.

"Yes," She murmured wiping her eyes. "Where am I?"

"You're on I-95 it looks like you ran off the road and hit that pole. Are you hurt?"

"No. I don't think so." Latrease reached for the ignition and tried to start the car.

"It's dead. The battery must've died out. I can give you a jump if you have cables; mine are in my other car. Or a ride and you can have a tow truck pick up your car in the morning if you like."

Latrease pulled the key out.

"Unless you have someone you want to call…" The stranger said looking in the car. It was dark. There was no light on the highway other than the glare coming from the headlights in the car behind her. She could see them reflecting in her mirrors. Latrease looked up at the man standing next to her door.

"No, I'll take the ride; let me get my things."

"I'm Randy, by the way, Dr. Randy Jackson." Latrease stuck her hand out the window to meet his.

"Latrease Wilson, nice to meet you, Dr. Jackson."

"You can call me Randy, though."

"Ok."

Latrease pushed the button to let her window up and then remembered the battery was dead. She grabbed her purse, opened the door and got out of her 1995 Honda Accord. When she tried to stand up she stumbled.

"Are you ok?" Randy caught her just before she fell. She was wearing a silver dress with shining rhinestones that sparkled from the reflection of his headlights. She was dressed like a superstar even though her makeup was smeared and she looked pale. Her hair was up with curly bangs. She was wearing what looked like very expensive jewelry even though her car appeared a bit beat up.

"No I'm not."

"Are you in pain? Is there anyone you want me to call?"

"No everybody important is dead. I don't have nobody to call, nobody at all." She snapped and slammed the door to the car.

Randy helped her back to his car, he opened the passenger door and she slid in. He then walked back over to her Honda Accord and locked the doors.

"Where do you live?"

"I don't wanna go home. Anywhere else but home."

The drive up the highway was quiet. Randy wondered what was wrong with the woman. She was beautiful, young.

"So this whole time you couldn't remember anything about yourself?" Shanice asked her sister.

"No." Latrease sighed.

"That had to be hard. How did you know you could trust him? I mean, I don't think I would've come home from the hospital with some total stranger like that." Shanice put the last dress on a hanger and hung it in the closet.

"I just did. It just felt like the thing to do. I didn't have a lot of options, you know." Latrease replied. She watched as her sister put the rest of the new baby clothes in the dresser.

"Yeah, but I've known you like forever and you ain't never been the one to just go somewhere with a stranger. Now me, on the other hand, you know me; I would've went just because he had cute eyes, but not you sister dearest. I'm just saying, it's a good thing he didn't turn out to be some fake psychiatrist, raping murderer."

"Oh my God, Niecy, don't talk like that. It's cool, we are cool and he ain't, he's the father of my child, the love of my life."

"Yeah, yeah, you told me that already. I'm just saying, just being me. You know I have never been one to sugar coat."

"Yes I know that." Latrease fluffed the pillows and stacked them against the headboard so she could sit up a little.

"Did it hurt?" Shanice sat on the end of the bed and started opening the packaged sets of onesies and folding them.

"Did what hurt?"

"Having the baby. Was it as painful as everybody says it is?"

"Yes, it was horrible. I thought I was gonna die." Latrease chuckled, "No actually I had an epidural so there was no pain at all."

"Oh…what's an epidural?"

"It's a shot they gave me in my spine. It makes you numb. I couldn't feel the pain. It *was* painful afterward, when the doctor was pressing on my stomach to get the after birth out, I wanted to scream. I would do it all over for this little beautiful girl in a heartbeat."

Latrease lie back on the pillow and grabbed her breasts. "Ouch."

"What's wrong sis?"

"My breasts feel like they are going to pop."

"Oh my they are mighty full and look like muscles. Are you breastfeeding?"

"No."

"So what's gonna happen to the milk if you don't let Keyana drink it."

"It's supposed to dry up. They are so sore, oh my goodness this is the worst feeling that I have ever felt." Latrease held her hands against her breasts. "Can you get me that ice pack from the freezer?"

"Sure, I will. Do you want me to call Randy?" Shanice walked over to the bedroom door and stopped.

"What for?"

"You said he was a doctor right?"

"He's not that kinda doctor and no I don't want to see him right now."

"Why not? I thought you two were…"

"Niecy, it's complicated. I don't wanna talk about it ok?"

"Alright."

Latrease watched as her sister left the room. She wondered how long Shanice was planning on being in town. It had been two hours since they'd been talking and she was already getting that funny vibe from her. The vibe she always got when she knew her sister was up to no good. Latrease knew it was a matter of time before her sister asked her for some money. She knew it would be a matter of time before her sister spilled that she didn't have anywhere to go.

Latrease remembered the last time she'd seen her sister. *It was a week after their parent's funeral. The family attorney, Mr. Clark, had requested certain family members attend the reading of the will. Shanice showed up thirty minutes late in a drunken stupor. She was wearing a sleezy red cocktail dress, eight inch pumps, and a gold tennis bracelet that she had stolen from Latrease's bedroom at their parents' house.*

"Sorry I'm late. I forgot this thing was today." Was all she said as she slid into the seat next to Latrease.

"So...what do we get?" Shanice slumped over the table. Stretching her right arm out and holding her face with her left hand.

"He hasn't started yet because we were waiting on you." Latrease sighed.

"Oh ok. Well let's get to it then my ride is circling the block so he won't have to pay that dumb parking meter." Shanice grunted.

"Are you seriously gonna disrespect mom and dad like this Niecey? Look at you, you didn't have the decency to take a shower and wash the sex funk off you before coming here. You are so disgusting. I bet mom is rolling..."

"Blah blah blah, rolling in her grave wishing it was me that died instead of them right? Is that what you wish sister deary? You hate me because I survived and mom and dad didn't! I am so tired..."

SMACK!

Latrease slapped her sister in the face with the palm of her hand.

"I'm sorry, Niecy." She tried to embrace her but Shanice pulled back.

"You know something, I am sorry this happened. I wish there was something I could do to change it but there isn't." Shanice wiped the tears that raced down her face away.

"I know that Niecy."

"No, no, no, let me finish. I am sorry that I don't grieve the way you do. But that doesn't mean I don't miss them. That doesn't mean I ain't crying myself to sleep every night. Anyway who the heck are you to tell me how I am supposed to grieve. Where were you the night it happened? You know if it wasn't for you and that dang play we wouldn't have been speeding up the highway in the first place. Where were you that night?"

Shanice stood up, straightened the crease in her dress and shoved Latrease hard in the chest.

"Who the heck do you think you are?"

"Shanice you are drunk. Sit down please." Latrease tried helping her sister back in her seat.

"Where the heck was you, Treasie? I mean, all night and the next few days. Where were you? Do you know how hard that was for me? Having to make arrangements to bury both my parents by myself while you were off doing God knows what, with God knows who. Then you show up at the funeral with some man I never saw before."

"I'm sorry Niecey. I'm sorry I wasn't there to help you."

"I am so tired of hearing how sorry everybody is!" Shanice slammed her hand on the table and sat back down.

"Young ladies calm down. This is neither the time nor place…"

"And why are you even here Aunt Gwen? You didn't even come to your own sisters' funeral!" Shanice stood up and walked over to the door.

"This is a joke. I'm outta here." She slammed the door behind her.

"Niecy wait!" Latrease ran after her but it was too late by the time she made it to the door that led outside Shanice was closing the door to the black Volvo and the car sped down the street.

Ding Dong. Randy put the dry dishes in the rack and walked over to the front door. "Who is it?"

"It's Shanice, Treasie's sister."

"Just a minute." Randy rushed to the bedroom and slipped his feet into his sandals. He then grabbed the television remote and changed the station.

"Come on in." he said as he sat down on the couch.

"Thanks." Shanice walked in slowly looking around the room. She was wearing a yellow tank top with a pair of cut off blue jean shorts. Her hair was pulled back in a ponytail. A few curls sprinkled across her face.

"Hi."

"Hi miss lady how are you?" Randy patted his hand on the couch motioning for her to sit down.

"I'm doing well."

"Come on over I don't bite." He told her.

Shanice shivered as she rubbed her hands up and down her arms.

"Are you cold?"

"It's a bit chilly."

Randy walked over to the thermostat on the wall and adjusted it.

"I'm sorry I'm so use to it just being me here and I get hot pretty quick."

"It's ok you don't have to change anything because of me," she sighed.

"It's fine, not a big deal at all. My mom hates coming over here because she says it's too hot; believe it or not." Randy walked back over and sat on the love seat. Shanice sat in the recliner.

"So you're the guy Treasie brought to our parents funeral, I remember seeing you then."

"Yes but I don't remember seeing you at all."

"You guys didn't stay long enough. Had you stayed you would have definitely saw me."

"I didn't know Latrease had a sister, let alone a twin sister, until yesterday when we got home from the hospital."

"I don't understand that. I mean, I've heard of amnesia but not like this."

"She has never told me about you. I thought she was an only child as a matter of fact that is what she told me."

"Oh my, God! I need to talk to you about her. Is she alright now?"

"She must have been suffering post-partum depression after your parents' accident. You know, she didn't tell me about the accident until the day before the funeral. Before that she acted as if nothing was wrong."

"How long did you know her before my parents died?"

"We met the same night, the night of their accident."

"*Our* accident, I was the one driving the car." Shanice eyes filled with tears. She wiped her face with her hand but it didn't stop the tears from flowing.

"Oh my, I am so sorry to hear that. Here, let me get you a Kleenex." Randy walked into the kitchen and grabbed the box from the pantry. He realised now that Latrease was having a break down the night he'd met her. He realised that this was not her first time suffering AMD. That she had also suffered it when her parents died. She had forced herself to forget her sister. Why he hadn't observed this back then, he wondered.

"Well I guess that explains why you never tried to find me." Shanice grabbed the tissue from the box and wiped her face.

"Yes. Latrease told me there wasn't any other family." Randy replied.

"In your professional opinion do you think she needs to be seen by someone else? I mean, no disrespect to you but someone that specialises in treating amnesia patients, because I am a bit lost here."

"Yes I do. I have someone that I will talk to and see if he can get her in his office."

"Ok, so what are you two going to do now?"

"Honestly, Shanice, I don't know."

"Call me Niecy. What do you mean, you don't know? You have to have a plan?"

"Don't get me wrong, I love your sister and I want to be there for our daughter, but right now I don't know what the right thing for me to do *is*."

"I don't understand."

"Your sister is pissed off at me right now. I don't know what to do. I tried to call her a few hours ago she said she was napping and she would call me back. I've been cleaning and trying to do as much as I can to stop myself from being tempted to call her back or go back there."

"Oh my, I don't know what to say."

"Would you like something to drink?" Randy asked.

"No. I think I better get back to the house. If it's alright with you I would like to stick around for a while, and help her with the baby."

"You are welcome to stay as long as you want. I am so glad my sister ran into you. It's good to have someone around that grew up with her."

"I will do everything I can to help. She *is* my sister after all."

Latrease poured the formula into the bottle and placed it in the boiling water. She waited thirty seconds and removed it. After pouring a few drops of milk on her hand she put the bottle back in the water for a few more seconds.

"Just right." She mumbled twisting the top back on the bottle. She walked into the living room and handed the bottle to her sister, who was holding Keyana.

"She has your ears and Randy's eyes."

"Yeah I guess."

Latrease sat down on the loveseat and grabbed one of the parenting magazines from the coffee table. "She is very special Niecy. I just wish mother and dad, could be here to see her."

"Yeah me too. I know they are looking down at her from Heaven though." Shanice smiled caressing the baby's hair from her forehead.

"I think it's cool that her hair has that brownish red thing going on."

"Yeah, I don't know where that came from."

"Well you know all of daddy's sisters had brownish red hair. That's probably where it came from." Shanice held the baby on her shoulder and started patting on her back to burp her.

"I don't mean to be nosey…"

"Then don't." Latrease snapped, slammed the magazine on the table and walked towards the kitchen door.

"Treasie, I wasn't trying to upset you, I just wanted to ask…"

"I don't wanna hear your questions. I don't care what you think of me, and I don't need your freaking advice. So why don't you just go back wherever you came here from and leave me alone."

"Latrease, calm down. I just wanted to ask what you were going to do about Randy?"

Latrease walked over and knelt down in front of her sister. "That is none of your business. Just like my life is none of your business. Why don't we get to the real issue? Like why are you here?"

"I'm trying to help you."

"Yeah, well I didn't ask for your help, did I?"

"Treasie what is wrong with you, why so much anger?"

"I'm angry because I am tired of people using me." Latrease sat on the love seat and yawned.

"What? Who's using you? I'm trying to help you Treasie, nobody is against you." Shanice held the baby up, laid her against her shoulder and began rubbing her back.

"I talked to Randy. He thinks you are mad at him still. Are you?"

"That is none of your business Niecy and I don't need your help."

"What is wrong with you Latrease Rene' Wilson?"

"Nothing I'm just stressed I guess. I'm sorry, Niecy. I am happy you are here. I don't know what I would do if you weren't." Latrease sat on the couch next to her sister.

"I'm gonna lay her in the bassinet and then we can have a cup of coffee and a nice chat in the kitchen." Latrease watched as her sister laid the baby on the blanket and walked into the kitchen.

Latrease poured the coffee in the cups and added sugar and cream. She sat at the table and waited for her sister to join her.

"I don't know what to say Shanice. I don't know what to do."

"I'm here for you Latrease, you are my sister. That's what sisters are for."

"Niecy if you knew what I did…" Latrease burst into tears.

Randy Jackson stood in front of the mirror in his bedroom. "Man I look good." He murmured to himself placing the brush on the dresser. He was wearing a lavender dress shirt with black slacks and black freshly polished Stacy Adams. He was excited about his date with Latrease. He was more excited that she had agreed to go out with him in the first place. He'd made reservations at a popular restaurant that had a live jazz band.

It had been two weeks since Keyana was born. Randy had started back taking patients that week. He had spoken with Dr. Jefferson about Latrease's condition. Dr. Jefferson had agreed to see her, now Randy had to convince Latrease that she needed to be evaluated by him. He knew this would be a challenge that he wasn't planning on tackling just yet. He just wanted to enjoy the night with Latrease. Just the two of them, alone.

Ever since they'd brought the baby home from the hospital, he'd seen Latrease often, but there were always others around. Whether his mother, Shemeka or Bertha he never had time to talk to her alone. Then there was Shanice, who had practically moved in the guesthouse. With her there all the time it was even harder for him to approach Latrease. It was as if she was guarding her from him. He knew that was silly to think but he couldn't help feeling that way.

Randy grabbed his wallet and keys then headed out the door and around the yard towards the guesthouse. As he walked down the corridor he admired the patches of flowers that were starting to bloom. There were bushes that had blue carnations that were budding and yellow roses that lined the front of the guesthouse. The birdbath in the center of the yard was surrounded by lilies and honeysuckles.

Randy smiled as he listened to the crickets and birds in harmony. He had never paid much attention to the beautiful orchestra they made until Latrease pointed it out to him. Now every time he was out at night he wondered what type of song they were making.

It was a cool spring night, the stars were sprinkled across the sky and the fireflies lit up the yard sporadically. Randy walked up the steps and stopped at the window. He watched as Latrease twirled around modelling her dress in front of her sister. She was wearing a peach colored dress that lay perfectly across her perky breasts. Randy admired the way her breasts looked gorgeous in that dress. Her hips hypnotised him; drawing him into her sensual dance.

"How do I look?" He heard her ask her sister.

"Beautiful. I won't wait up for you."

"Puh-lease, this is just going to be dinner and conversation. Nothing more, nothing less." Latrease slid her arm into the sweater.

"That's only because of mother nature. I know if you didn't have to wait six weeks after giving birth, tonight you would probably rape poor Randy." Shanice giggled and Randy realized she knew he was standing there.

"Hi brutha- in- law." She giggled again.

"Hi ladies."

Randy opened the screen door, walked over and gave Shanice a hug. Then he fixed his attention on Latrease. She was beautiful. She had straightened out her hair and was wearing it down. Randy had never seen her hair without curls before. He was immediately aroused.

He wrapped his arms around her, inhaling the intoxicating fragrance of her perfume, and hair spray. She felt good in his arms. Her skin was soft against his face. He couldn't remember the last time he had held her so close.

"You look awesome." he whispered in her ear before she pulled away from the hug.

"Thank you. You're not so bad looking yourself." Both ladies giggled.

"Oh it's like that, huh?" Randy smiled and did a slow spin so the girls could check him out.

"Oh dang, he got the ol school Stacy Adams on and everything." Shanice bent down and touched the front of the shoe.

"Oh, you sharp alright."

Latrease and her sister slapped each others hand in the air as if giving a high-five. Randy wasn't sure if they were agreeing that he looked good or calling him old fashioned, but at least she was smiling and that was a good thing.

"You sure you can handle the baby, Niecy?" Latrease asked her sister.

"Yeah, girl I got this, go on with yo man and have some fun."

After filling up three bottles of milk and placing them in the fridge, Randy kissed Keyana on the forehead and laid her in the bassinet.

"Good night sweety, I love you." Latrease gave the baby a kiss on the cheek.

"Let's go before I change my mind."

She motioned Randy. He wondered what was going through her head. He knew this was the first time she'd be leaving the baby. He crossed his fingers behind his back as he escorted her out the door.

The drive to the restaurant was quiet. Randy started out by playing his R. Kelly CD; after two songs Latrease asked if she could look through his CD case.

"Ah man you have so many CD's I like. Can we listen to this one?"

Randy nodded. The first song began to play. It was a song by Aaliyah called, *The One I Gave My Heart To.*

"Of all songs." Randy murmured under his breath.

"Excuse me?" Latrease looked up from reading the CD cover.

"Nothing."

"I didn't hear you. What did you say?"

"I was just saying that I love hearing you sing this song."

"I've never sang this song to you, what are you talking about Randy?"

"I'm sorry, I meant to say you sound good singing it."

"What is up with you? You're so used to lying, the lies just roll off your tongue now, don't they?" she snapped.

"I didn't mean to..."

"Why Randy, why did you have to lie to me all these months?"

Randy pulled the car into the parking lot of the restaurant. After circling the lot he found a spot and parked.

"I had to. Latrease, you had amnesia. I couldn't tell you anything about your past, or you would have forgotten forever. I had to let you remember on your own."

"Yeah, yeah, you said that already. So if I would have never remembered you would have never told me?" she sighed, pulling the bangs behind her ear.

"It was hard as heck for me to not tell you. You have to believe me."

"So you were gonna let me go on looking for my child's father..."

"I'm her father..."

"You were just gonna let me think I was alone."

"No, Treasie I was gonna be there for you and Keyana every minute of the way."

"While we lived in your guesthouse right?"

"No. I don't know. What do you want me to say?" Randy felt a lump in his throat as big as a tennis ball. He couldn't swallow.

"What I want you to say? I want you to say a lot of things. Will you say them? Probably not, so it doesn't matter what I want you to say." she snapped and unbuckled her seatbelt.

"Latrease I'm trying. Can you give me *that*? I am trying. I want to be there for you and our daughter. I wanna be the best dad I can be for her."

"Yeah, like you are with your son. *What,* you see him like twice a month now right? Is that you being the best dad that you can be?"

"It's complicated Latrease, you don't know Valerie..."

"I know enough about her now. Your sister told me all about how she gave birth and married another man, because you wouldn't step up to the plate."

"That's not true, Valerie and I were not in love. I didn't have feelings for her..."

"Yeah just like you don't have feelings for me!"

"Oh my God. Latrease you are really making this hard for me."

"*I'm* making it hard on *you*?"

"Yes, you are. I'm trying to fix this. You bringing up Valerie and Keyon and they don't have anything to do with this." Randy turned the car off and removed the key from the ignition.

"So how do you plan to fix this Randy?"

"Well I do want you to see a specialist who works with amnesia patients. I've already talked to a colleague of mine about seeing you..."

"*That's* your plan? Send me to another shrink so y'all can continue to play with my head for another few months?"

"I want to get you some help..."

"I don't need anymore help. I am just fine. I remember everything. Especially the part where you don't want a relationship with me. So here's *my* plan, I will get back to work and be out of your way in a few months."

"Latrease listen..."

"For what...there's nothing else to say. Are we gonna eat or what?"

Randy watched as Latrease got out of the car and grabbed her handbag. He had never seen her this feisty. This rebellious. If it wasn't for the fact that she was rebelling against *him*, this side of her would have definitely turned him on.

Randy grabbed his wallet from inside the glove compartment. Then got out and walked over to meet Latrease who was standing in front of the Mercedes Benz.

"It's a bit chilly, do you want my jacket?", he asked.

"No, I'm ok. Look Randy I'm sorry. I didn't mean to come off like a...well you know. Let's just eat and enjoy ourselves tonight."

Randy felt a wave of relief come over him. He smiled and leaned in to give her a hug. As he held her in his arms he realized he wanted to spend the rest of his life with her. It was at that moment that he knew she was the one for him.

"Listen." Latrease looked up into his eyes.

"I think it's a love song. A sweet gentle love song. I think they knew we would be here tonight." Randy listened as the birds sang and the crickets chirped in melody.

"No, I was talking about that sound my belly just made. I'm starving."

They both laughed.

Latrease gazed at the menu. Her belly continued rumbling as she smelled all the food around her. She wondered if she would be able to make a good decision being that she was so hungry. Randy had ordered an appetizer platter for them to share; that included four mini cheeseburgers, bacon wrapped grilled shrimp, and southwestern eggrolls.

"Would you like to try a white wine sample tonight?" The young blonde waitress asked while holding up a bottle.

"I would love some." Latrease smiled at the lady.

"I'll have a sample too." Randy told the girl, who then poured the wine in two glasses and sat them on the table. Latrease took a sip and swished it around her mouth. It was sweet and fruity.

"That was nice." she told Randy and continued looking over the menu.

"Do you want me to get us a bottle?" he asked.

"Maybe a small one." she replied.

Latrease held her finger on the the dish on the menu that she wanted to order so that she wouldn't lose it's place.

"That music is lovely." she whispered.

"Yes it is."

"Maybe if you're feeling up to it, we can dance later." He drew closer.

Randy was looking good. She had to admit to herself that he was sharp. She knew he would be though. He'd always been good at dressing to impress and he was definitely impressing her. She just didn't want him to know it. Not yet anyway.

It felt good having the tables turned. She could clearly see that Randy's feelings for her had grown stronger. She could see the love in his eyes when they quarrelled in the car. She just didn't want to give in yet. She wanted to stretch it out a bit. Besides there was still that one other issue.

"Do you know what you want to order, or do you guys need a little more time." The waitress asked, and pulled a pencil and pad out from her apron.

"Yes we're ready." Randy replied.

"Ok what can I get you sir?"

"I'll have the New York Strip, steamed veggies and the baked potato with butter and sour cream."

The lady scribbled on the notepad and then looked up.

"Would you like a tossed salad or caesar salad with your meal sir?"

"No salad for me, thank you."

She then looked at Latrease.

"I'll have the combo deal with the half rack of baby back bbq ribs and the fried chicken tenders. I'll also take a Caesar Salad and homemade mashed potatoes."

"Wow, Treasie you sure you can eat all that? Remember you're not eating for two anymore."

Latrease rolled her eyes. "Yes I can eat it. I am starving." She placed the napkin in her lap.

What was *his* problem, she wondered. Who did he think he was, telling her how much she could eat. Latrease reminisced on the morning after she'd met Randy. He had taken her to a restaurant for breakfast. She had ordered eggs, hashbrowns, grits, pancakes, bacon, sausage, and toast. He had told her he didn't think she could eat it all. She'd insisted she would, so they made a bet. If she ate all of her breakfast he would have to cook her dinner. If she didn't eat it all she would have to cook him dinner. She'd lost.

"Here's your salad and croutons."

"Thank you."

Latrease ate some of the appetizers and listened to the music. The restaurant was dim lit and decorated nicely. There was a nice flower arrangement in the middle of the table.

"Hmm. How about we make a little wager?" Randy asked after the waitress placed the main courses on the table.

"I'm listening." Latrease looked across the table at Randy.

"If you don't eat everything off your plate you have to give me a good night kiss."

Latrease felt the blood rush to her cheeks. She tried to hold in her smile but she couldn't. He was looking quite attractive. It had always been hard to resist his charms but now she knew she had to fight hard. She didn't want to fall down in the same hole she'd been in with him before.

"What do *I* get when *you* lose?" She picked up the knife and spread butter on her roll.

"*If* you win you can drive my car out to the city and have a day at the spa. I'll bring Keyana up to the house with me and you can enjoy a full day at the spa when you are feeling better." He looked down at his watch.

"Hmm."

"Let's say May, 13th how does that sound?" Latrease smiled. Randy was definitely laying it on thick. How could she ever refuse such a deal?

"I accept." she grinned and started her meal. Eating in front of Randy had never been a problem for her. When she dated guys in the past she'd had problems eating in front of them. There was something different about Randy. Something that made her feel comfortable.

That night was different. It was like being in high school on a first date. Every time she would put the fork to her mouth she felt giddy and put it back down. Twenty minutes later she surrendered.

"I can't believe this. I was so hungry. After those appetizers and bread I think I got full or something."

Randy smiled and asked the waitress to remove the dishes.

"If it's alright with you can we just sit here for a while and listen to the music," she asked.

"Yes, sure."

The drive back to the house was romantic. Randy was playing an Al Green CD. Latrease smiled everytime Randy tried to sing. It was hilarious to her. Singing was definitely not a gift he possessed. She never let him hear her laugh though.

"I don't know if it was the wine or the music but I am so wide awake right now, it ain't even funny."

"Me neither. You wanna watch some television?"

"Sure." Latrease felt a tingle down her spine when Randy grabbed her hand to help her out of the car. She knew she probably shouldn't stay and watch a movie with him but she wasn't ready for the night to end just yet. It felt so good being with him. Just the two of them without her sister or his family all in their face trying to be nosy.

"Maybe there's a good scary movie on?" she told him.

Latrease and Randy entered the house through the garage. She immediately felt the cold air hit her arms.

"Are you cold?"

"Yes, how did you know?"

"You're always cold when you come here." he walked over to the thermostat to adjust the temperature. What's gotten into you, she asked herself. Why was she reading so much into everything. Latrease looked around the room.

When she saw the island in the middle of the kitchen; she suddenly felt like there was a huge lump in her throat. There was a vase with beautiful flowers in it. There was a card and from that far away Latrease could read "You mean the world to me. R.J." She wanted to run out of the house.

"I don't feel so good, Randy. I think I will just go home and get some sleep."

"Huh, I thought we were gonna watch a movie."

"Yeah, I know. I'm sorry, maybe another time." She tried to hold back the tears that had formed in her eyes. She didn't want him to see them. She just wanted to leave. How could he? How could he bring another woman to his home? How could he after she had just given birth to his child only two weeks ago.

"What's wrong? You were fine just a minute ago? Do you need to go to the Emergency Room?"

She bit down on her lower lip.

"No, I just need to get out of here." Latrease rushed to the door and was in the garden in seconds. She could hear Randy calling out to her, but she did not stop running. Her legs were weak. She felt something snag her dress. She reached down to see what it was. A thorn from the rose bush pricked her finger.

"Ouch."

"Latrease, wait."

"I'm going to bed, Randy, leave me alone please."

"Leave you alone? Are you serious? See, this is what I can't stand about you. One minute you act all mature and the next..."

"Oh, so I'm acting childish? Well, maybe, that's because I'm only *twenty one*." she snapped.

"Oh my goodness, Latrease. This has nothing to do with your age."

"Yeah, well maybe your new woman won't act childish and y'all will live happily ever after. I'm outta here."

She put her finger in her mouth and sucked the blood. Then continued up the walk to the porch of the guesthouse.

"What *new* woman?" Randy ran behind her.

"The one who forgot to take her flowers with her last night."

Randy grabbed Latrease's hand.

"Sweety, those flowers are for you. I wanted to surprise you with them tonight. There is no other woman. You are the only woman in my life."

"If they're for me then why didn't you give them to me when you came to get me?"

"I wanted to..."

"Oh my goodness Randy you have become a habitual liar. I don't believe anything that comes out of your mouth anymore."

"I wanted to give them to you, I just forgot to grab them when I was on my way back here. I can prove it. I have the giftcard for the spa day for you on May 13th in the card envelope. It already has your name and everything on it."

"Are you serious?"

"Yes." Latrease looked in Randy's eyes. She knew he was telling the truth just by looking at him.

"Why did you pick May 13th?"

"Because your six weeks will be up on May 12th, so I thought you would enjoy a relaxing day of pampering."

"Wow."

He grabbed her hand.

"Well I owe you an apology, I'm sorry I accused you of lying."

She gazed into his eyes as he pulled her closer and leaned in for a kiss. She felt the flutter of butterflies in her stomach. She wrapped her arms around him, caressing his back as their tongues danced the tango. In that moment, Latrease knew she was very much in love with Randy. It felt different than any other time they'd kissed before. She knew he was in love with her too.

A few minutes later, Randy was still holding her.

"I love you, Latrease."

She felt the blood rush to her cheeks again. Randy had never said those words to her before. It felt weird hearing him say them to her, yet it felt so right.

"I love you too, Randy.

"I see you had a good time last night." Shanice knocked on the door to the bathroom.

"You can come in." Latrease told her. "Why you say that?" Latrease traced her lips with a black liner then applied a shiny gloss to them.

"Well you didn't get home until...umm a few minutes after 6am." Shanice walked into the bathroom. She was wearing a black satin gown that had lace around the edges with a matching robe.

"That looks familiar." Latrease pointed to the gown.

"Mom gave it to me. Don't change the subject." she giggled.

"Well if you must know we did have a nice evening." Latrease smiled. She brushed her hair up and wrapped a ponytail holder around it.

"Ahh, so where did ya go?"

"We went to this fancy restaurant called 'Lovelys', they had a live band and everything."

"Ooh sounds romantic." Shanice sat on the edge of the bath tub.

Latrease jumped as she heard the phone ring.

"I'll get it." Shanice scrambled to the living room to answer the phone. Latrease finished up with her hair.

"It's for you."

"Who is it?"

"I think she said Valerie."

"Ugh, what the heck does she want?" Latrease grabbed the phone and went into the living room.

"Hello."

"Hi is this Treasie?"

"Yes it is, how may I help you?" Latrease recalled the last time she'd seen Valerie. How she had left Randy's son with her and went out of town.

"Hi this is Valerie, we met once at Randy's house a few months ago. Do you remember?"

"Yes of course."

"Well my son has been going on and on about having a baby sister that lives in his daddy's guesthouse. I thought he was lying until I ran into Shemeka earlier today and she confirmed it." Shanice walked into the living room and looked at Latrease as if to say 'who's that'.

"Yes that's true."

"My thing is this, I don't know what kinda games you and Randy are playing, but when you start lying to my child then it's a problem for me..."

"Excuse me, but I haven't lied to your child..."

"I wasn't finished. You told him that he was going to be able to come over and see his new baby sister and that's all he talks about is his sister that's named after him. He ain't seen that baby or Randy since she was born."

Shanice came closer and sat on the couch next to Latrease.

"I apologize, I have been very busy dealing with everything and my sister is here and it's just been overwhelming."

"Well, I can understand that. At least *you* have some help. Randy didn't do squat for me when Keyon was a baby. Other than writing those checks. They weren't even enough to do much with. You know he makes over three hundred thousand dollars a year and all he gives me is three thousand dollars a month. What am I supposed to do when he starts school this fall. That won't barely cover his tuition and room and board."

"Tuition? He will only be in kindergarten right?"

"Yes and it costs close to nine thousand dollars per year."

"Well, maybe he should go to public school. It's free." Latrease rolled her eyes.

"I didn't call you to ask your advice on raising my child. My child will not be going to a public school with all those rug rats and rift raft. Do you see me giving you advice on lets see, why you living in the guesthouse instead of the main house? No you do not!"

Latrease wanted to hang the phone up. Who did this woman think she was? What made her think she had a right to call yelling and trash talking?

"Hey Valerie, I have to go. You need to talk to Randy not me."

Latrease placed the phone on the receiver, took a deep breath and exhaled.

"Wow, sounds like you got baby mama drama." Shanice giggled.

"Yeah, well I'ma nip this in the bud,real quick, fast, and in a hurry." she replied.

The phone rang again. Latrease picked it up after the second ring.

"Hello"

"Hey Treasie it's Shemeka, look, I saw Valerie at the gas station today and she asked me a million..."

"Yeah, I know, she just called me."

"Wanna do lunch?"

"Sure."

"I'll pick you up at noon ok, you can take the baby up to mama's she don't mind watching her, that way your sister can come too."

"Ok. we'll be ready."

Latrease placed the phone on the receiver and turned to her sister.

"You wanna go to lunch with Shemeka and me?"

"Who?"

"Randy's sister. The one who saw you at the drivers license place."

"Yeah, sure. Let me get dressed." Shanice went in the other bedroom to get ready. Latrease started packing a diaper bag for the baby. She then called to make sure it was ok to bring her.

A few minutes later they were on their way through the garden to the front of Honey Grove Circle. It was warm and sunny. They were dressed alike in outfits Shanice had bought for them when she went to the mall with Kevin and Calvin the weekend before.

"Good morning, Miss Bessie." Latrease gave Randy's mom a hug and took the baby out of the sling and handed her to the woman.

"Good morning, and how is my granddaughter?"

"She's good." Latrease replied.

"How are you ladies? You look so much alike it's hard to tell which is who." they all giggled.

Randy looked through the glass of the counter then motioned for the sales lady to aid. "I like this one, can I see it?" he asked.

"Oh that's a nice one." the short brunette opened the case and pulled the ring out. She handed it to Randy. After admiring it for a few minutes he told the lady he wanted it.

"This is definitely the one."

The lady smiled.

"Well, she is a lucky lady to have a man willing to spend five thousand dollars on an engagement ring."

"It's not actually going to be an engagement ring. It's a promise ring."

The lady raised her brow.

"What do you mean 'promise ring'?"

"I'm not asking her to marry me. I just want her to know that I will always be there for her. She's been through a lot and I want her to know she can count on me."

"I see. My husband had that same problem."

"What problem?" Randy stood up straight.

"Commitment issues. Frankly, the thought of committing scared the mess out of him."

Randy scratched his head.

"So, what happened?"

"I ended up dating someone else. He sat by and watched me date another guy. He literally stalked us. Everywhere we went he showed up. It was crazy. Finally one night after he watched the guy walk me home, he knocked on my mothers door and asked me to come outside. He had a ring in his hand. He got down on one knee and asked me to marry him."

"Sounds kinda romantic."

"Not really, because the guy I was dating turned around and came back. I had left my purse in his car. When he saw George, that's his name, down on one knee proposing, he attacked him."

"Oh my goodness."

"Yeah, he beat the crap outta George." The sales clerk put her hand on her hip.

"Well, I know there was a happy ending somewhere in there."

"Yeah, he ended up getting fifteen stitches on his face. He was in the hospital for three days. I went to visit him the night before he got out and I accepted his proposal. I brought the justice of the peace with me. Til this day he will say, those two weeks that I dated Johnny, were the sickest time of his life."

"That's crazy." Randy wiped the sweat from his forehead.

"Yeah, if you love her what's stopping you?" The older lady put her hand on her hip.

"I don't know. Me I guess." Randy took his checkbook out of his wallet.

"I want the ring in size 8, If I get it inscribed how long will it take?"

The woman leaned over the counter, Randy could smell her perfume.

"Son if you're gonna give her *this* ring you better be ready for more than a promise."

"I think I am." Randy smiled, jotted down what he wanted inscribed in the ring and signed the check.

A few minutes later Randy was in his car on the way back to the office. It had been a slow morning, he'd only had two patients before lunch.

"Your one thirty cancelled. The mom says the school is in the middle of state testing. I rescheduled for next week." Armentha looked up long enough to see Randy nod and then continued typing.

"So have you heard back from Dr. Jefferson?"

"Yes, he said he can see her Thursday at ten."

"Ok sounds good."

Armentha stopped typing. "Can I talk to you for a minute?"

"Sure, what's on your mind?"

"You know, Dr Jackson, I've never been one to get in your business; but I do think you are doing the right thing by having a specialist work with Latrease. That is, if *she* wants that. I've never judged you about the way you handled her situation. Personally I would have preferred her know who I was, than her suffer the way she did."

Randy sat down in the chair facing her desk.

"I'm not a doctor I'm just a secretary so of course I have no knowledge of what's best in these situations. I do like Latrease a lot and she seems like a great girl. I wish you too the best, whatever that may be."

"Thank you, Armentha. I hate the way things went."

"Yeah but she's strong. I'm sure the two of you will be fine. Is there anything I can do for you?"

"Not right now. I will let you know if I need something."

"Ok."

Randy spent the next few hours going over paperwork in his office. He wasn't expecting a call from Latrease so when the phone rang and his name showed up on the caller id box he was surprised.

"Hi there."

"Hi Randy, we need to talk. Valerie called..."

"Ugh, I'm sorry. I didn't know she had that number. What did she want?"

"She wants you to spend more time with your son. She wants him to see the baby. She wants you to pay nine thousand dollars for him to go to private school. She wants a lot of stuff that has nothing to do with me Randy."

"I don't know why she called you. She knows the number here and she knows my pager number too. I will handle this when I get home."

"Ok. Can I get the key to the shed. I wanna get some of my stuff out and look through and see what I want to get rid of."

"Sure. Mama has a copy, you can get it from her or wait til I get there and I can help."

Randy sighed.

"I will call your mother and get if from her. Shemeka already said she would come over and help. Bertha too. So I will have plenty of help. How's your day going so far?"

"It's pretty slow. I had a few cancellations today. I was wondering if maybe we could catch a movie or something later."

"Hmm, I'll let you know ok."

Later that evening Latrease was sitting in a lounge chair in the backyard while the others carried her things out of the shed. She was wearing some blue jean cut off shorts and a white t-shirt. Her sister was sitting in the swing on the porch. Keyana was in her bassinet sleeping.

"This is so pretty Latrease." Bertha held up a painting of an angel watching over a boy and a girl as they walked over a bridge.

"Yeah my mom gave me that. I had some lamps that matched it but one of them got broke."

"Ahh, I know how it feel for something like that to happen to things you cherish. When the boys were toddlers I couldn't have anything nice."

"Yeah well my sister came over drunk one night and fell over the couch, her arm knocked the lamp on the floor and it shattered."

"Shanice drunk?"

"Yes."

"That's hard to believe. She seems so sweet." Bertha replied.

"Yes, that's because she wants to seem that way."

"Wow."

"I wanna throw those curtains away." Latrease told Shemeka then pointed to a box.

"Can you bring me that box?" Shemeka carried the box over to Latrease and sat it down beside her. Latrease pulled her hair behind her ears. Her curls had come back after she'd taken a shower earlier.

"I have so much junk that needs throwing away."

Shemeka smiled.

"Well you have all the time in the world to look through this stuff and figure out what you want to do with it."

Latrease laughed and looked through the box of compact disc's. As she picked through them she felt a shiver run through her spine when she held up the Celine Dion cover. There were so many songs on that album that she loved hearing.

Bertha walked over, looked down at Latrease and smiled.

"I'm not trying to be nosy but what exactly are you planning on doing. I mean are you and my brother in law together or..."

"I don't know Bertha. It's too soon to know what this really is. I mean don't get me wrong I love Randy with all my heart but I don't think he is ready for all that. He sure as heck wasn't before the accident."

"Ahh but I can tell from the way he is now. Whenever he comes to the gym it's like he has this glow about him." Bertha reached down in the box and pulled out more of the CD's.

"I was thinking about coming back to the gym a bit next week." Latrease said.

"Why? You're supposed to be resting and bonding with that beautiful little baby of yours."

"Yeah I know but I miss having something to do everyday other than change diapers, warm bottles, and listen to waah waah waah."

"Awe poor baby got the baby blues."

"I don't know about that I just need to get out of the house some. It gets boring sometimes."

"I can totally understand how you feel. When I had Calvin and Kevin I was put on bed rest for two months after they were born. Imagine that. Bernard's cooking was so awful he had to get his mom and dad to bring me a plate every time they cooked." Bertha picked up a VHS case that had some writing on it.

"Were you on Star Search?" Bertha asked, holding up the case.

"Yes, it was a long time ago. I was about twelve, I think."

"What did you do on there?"

"I sung 'THE GREATEST LOVE OF ALL', I won ten thousand dollars on that show."

"Wow, I would love to watch it."

"You can take it home and watch it, just make sure you bring it back ok."

"Ok I'll let the boys watch it with me."

A few hours later Latrease and Shanice were in the living room watching television while sorting through the clothes from the shed. To her surprise she could pretty much fit into her old clothes with no problem. The weight she'd gained from the pregnancy was all gone. She was happy to have her figure back. Even though she was back down to her size she still got tired fast.

"I'm gonna take a nap. I don't feel so good." Latrease went into her bedroom, and changed out of her shorts into a long night shirt.

"Here I'll get you some warm tea, it will help you relax." Shanice went into the kitchen and was back a few minutes later.

8 o'clock p.m. Randy grabbed the oven mitten and pulled the pan out. It was hot and the steam from the pan hit his face quick. The barbeque lamb chops smelled delicious. He placed the pan on the counter and started fixing the plates. He was so excited about having Latrease over for dinner. He wanted to show her his cooking skills. He put the plates on the counter and lit some candles around the room. The mood was set, he had soft music playing on the stereo.

He had a bouquet of carnations in a vase in the center of the table. Randy glanced at his watch. "She should be here any minute now," he thought. A few seconds later the doorbell rang.

When he opened the door his heart skipped a beat. She was so beautiful. She was wearing a black long body dress with shiny sparkling jewels that graced her body so wonderfully. She looked amazing. Her hair was up with a few curls sprinkled along her face. She was wearing shiny earrings and a choke that matched.

"You look gorgeous." he invited her in.

"Mmm something smells good." she said.

Randy grabbed her jacket and hung it on the coat rack. He motioned her to the dining room area and pulled the chair out for her. She sat down.

"I wanted to surprise you."

"Hmm so you got your mom to cook dinner and bring it over?" She giggled.

"No I cooked it all myself." Randy placed the plates on the table. He was proud of himself to have prepared such a great meal. Alongside the lamb-chops Randy had made homemade mashed potatoes, squash casserole, cornbread, and strawberry cheesecake for desert.

"Well I sure hope it tastes as good as it smells."

"Are you ok, you sound a bit..."

"Yeah my allergies are bothering me, it's because of all the pollen everywhere. It makes my voice sound a little throaty."

"Oh ok. I have some benadryl if you think it would help."

"No thanks, I will be ok." She cleared her throat.

Randy joined at the table and said grace. They ate and enjoyed the music. After dinner they sat on the loveseat in the living room and watched the movie: *I KNOW WHAT YOU DID LAST SUMMER.* Randy picked that movie because he knew how much Latrease liked the actress/singer Brandy.

"It's cold in here."

"Would you like me to turn down the air conditioning, or get you a blanket?"

"How about you get us a blanket." she replied and winked an eye. Randy was immediately aroused. He could feel the pulsating sensation from inside his pants.

When he returned with the blanket she was laying on the couch with her hair tossed on the pillow.

"Lay with me." she patted her hand on the couch motioning for him to join her. His heart raced. He spread the cover over her body and eased behind her on the couch.

"Kiss me daddy." she said and turned her body to face him. Her lips were soft, her kiss was hot. Nothing like the last time they'd kissed in the garden. There was something different about the way she kissed him this time. It was as if she wanted more. More than just a kiss.

She pressed her body closer, grinding against his erection. Her kisses were hot, hard. She wrapped her tongue around his and sucked and nibbled on his lip.

"You just don't know how much I love you." he whispered.

"Don't talk." she whispered back.

Randy kissed her ears, her neck, she started pulling her dress down to her feet. He slowly made his way down to her breasts.

"Mmm you taste so good."

He licked her breasts and teased her nipples with his hot tongue.

She grabbed his erection in her hand and massaged it gently. She continued throwing her body against his, harder and faster. Randy could feel heat between her legs.

"Mmm you feel so good."

"Shhh" she put her finger up to her lip. "Don't talk." she whispered.

Randy kissed her belly and noticed she was wearing a bellybutton ring, her bellybutton was never pierced before.

"Mmm when did you get this done?" he asked but she never replied.

"I want you Randy, make love to me."

She lifted her bottom a few inches and started pulling her thongs down.

He continued kissing her body while she reached to unbuckle his pants.

"Isn't it too soon, I mean you still have a few weeks before you can..."

"Latrease has a few weeks, I am ready for you inside me now." she giggled. Randy jumped up.

"What the ...?" Randy looked at the naked woman laying on the couch. It was *not* Latrease.

Shanice smiled a crooked smile. "What's the matter daddy? Cat got your tongue?"

"You tricked me..." Randy wiped the sweat from his face.

"I didn't trick you. You saw what you wanted to see."

"No. why are you here, where is your sister?"

"You invited me, remember. You called. I answered. You asked me over for dinner. I couldn't resist."

"I called your sister!"

"But you got me, on the phone and now right here in the flesh. Don't you still want me Randy?" She stood up and moved towards him. Smiling that wicked smile. She wrapped her arms and left leg around him.

"We can pretend I'm her. I don't mind. I've wanted to feel you inside me ever since the first time I saw you at the funeral. I knew you had to be a great catch because my sister ran off with you and never came back home."

Randy pushed her off him, grabbed the blanket and wrapped it around her.

"You need to get dressed. What is wrong with you?"

Shanice giggled, then threw the blanket down on the floor.

"Come on Randy, don't you want to feel my hot sweet lips wrapped around your..."

"Shanice you need to get dressed and leave." Randy picked the dress up from the floor and tried to hand it to her.

"But I don't want to. I wanna stay and play. Don't you wanna play with me Randy?" She swivelled her hip to the side and raised her leg up placing her foot on the arm of the couch.

"Don't you wanna come play inside?" she smiled.

"No, this is a mistake." Randy backed away from the woman. He buckled his pants. His mind was rambling. He couldn't think straight. What was this woman doing here? Why was she doing this? How could she disrespect her sister like this?

"Where's the bedroom?"

"Shanice you need to leave."

"No, I don't, I need to be in your bed. You need a hot sexy woman in your bed with you at night." she looked down at the bulge sticking out from his pants. "I know you been needing some tending to. I wanna be there for you. I wanna give you pleasure after pleasure, night after night."

She moved closer, grabbing him by the back of his neck, pulling him closer. She closed her eyes, kissed him on the lips.

"See this is fun, ain't it?"

"No. Shanice you have to go. We can't do this. I'm in love with your sister."

"Oh well you better hope she doesn't find out about this."

Shanice grabbed the dress and slid it over her head.

"I'd hate for her to leave and take that pretty little baby of yours away. The last I heard she was thinking of moving some place far far away. I'm pretty sure when she finds out her lover boy has been dry humping her twin sister, she's definitely gonna wanna be as far away from Georgia as she can."

"Oh my goodness Shanice, how can you be so cruel?" Randy watched as the woman teased about the room.

"Oh you ain't seen nothing yet. I think you might want me gone now, right?"

Randy nodded his head.

"Well that is gonna cost you. Somewhere along the line of twenty five thousand dollars. I can take a check. Do you need a pen?"

Randy could not believe this was happening. One minute he was having a wonderful evening with the woman he loved, the next he was being hustled out of twenty five grand.

"I am going to give you the money, but I want you gone tonight. I don't want you around here anymore do you understand?"

"Pinky swear." she put her pinky finger in her mouth and licked it.

Randy went into the kitchen and grabbed his checkbook from the drawer. He then wrote a check for twenty five thousand dollars. Shanice walked into the kitchen behind him.

"I need a ride to the airport."

"You can call a cab."

"Fine I can say goodbye to my sister and niece."

"No! I will take you. Let's go." Randy waved for her to come with him. They went through the kitchen to the garage and was in the Lexus in minutes.

The drive to the airport was quiet. Randy wanted to turn around, go home and confess everything to Latrease but he knew she would never forgive him. Maybe this was the best thing to do. He knew that Shanice was up to no good and maybe now that she had what she wanted she would disappear forever. His stomach felt like he'd been punched in it. He could barely concentrate.

"I need you to pay for my ticket. You know I can't get on a plane with a check right?"

Shanice glanced over at Randy as he parked the car.

"Where are you going, if you don't mind my asking?"

"Vegas. I am going to dance in Vegas." She got out of the car and they walked into the airport up to the customer service desk of one of the airlines.

"What time does your next flight leave to Vegas?"

The lady behind the desk looked in her computer then said, "In thirty minutes. The only seats I have available are window seats in coach. The ticket is three hundred seventy bucks. Would you like that flight?"

Shanice looked at Randy and grinned. "Yes, please."

"Ok are you both going or just one of you?", the lady asked.

"Just me, my sister would go crazy if I took her man to Vegas." she chuckled.

Randy was pissed. He wanted this woman on that plane and out of his life already.

"Ok I am going to need to see your identification card."

Shanice grabbed the drivers license from her purse and handed it to the lady. The customer service lady started typing in her computer and then handed the license back to Shanice.

Randy glanced over at Shanice who quickly put the license up in her purse.

"Ok that will be four hundred and ten dollars, how will you be paying?"

Shanice looked up at Randy.

"You got this right, brutha-in-law? Ha ha I can never get used to saying that."

That night, when he got back home, he couldn't sleep. All he could think about was what happened earlier. How he should have known it wasn't Latrease in the first place. How could he, though. She looked identical to Latrease. He knew that if he was gonna get Latrease to marry him, he would have to ask her soon.

Randy heard the phone ringing in the distance. He was drained. He could barely get his eyes opened. He'd drank a bottle of whiskey and was in a drunken stupor before finally falling asleep on the floor.

The phone continued to ring. Finally he got up and answered it.

"Randy, what is going on, why haven't you returned any of my calls?" Randy sat up on the couch.

"Who is this?"

"Oh, you don't know my voice anymore, now that you got your new baby mama in the backyard you forgot what I sound like?"

"Valerie, this is not the time..."

"When is the time? You haven't seen your son in God knows how long. What is your problem, Randy? And how come you ain't told me about your new baby? Why I have to find out through our son?"

"It was none of your business." Randy snapped.

"None of my business? I don't think so. None of my business, is why she staying in the guesthouse. That's none of my business. But when you take my son with you to the hospital while your little play thing gives birth to a baby, and you tell him that it's his baby sister, and you tell him not to tell the mother, and you tell him to lie...That *is* my business."

"Valerie, I know you're mad but now is not the time for this conversation."

"Well I'm on my way to your house right now. So you better make some time." Randy heard the phone being slammed on the hook, followed by the dial tone. He hated arguing with Valerie. He was not in the mood to talk to her. A few seconds later the phone rang again.

"Look, Valerie, I would prefer you not come over right now..."

"Randy my sister is missing." Randy could hear the panic in Latrease's voice. He felt like he'd been punched in the stomach.

"Latrease, calm down, why do you think she's missing?" He asked.

"She's not here. I can't find her. Nobody's seen her."

"Maybe she went out." Randy sighed.

"She doesn't go out without telling me."

"Calm down, I'm sure she's alright."

"Can you watch Keyana for a while I wanna try to find her?"

"Yes sure do you want me to come with you I can get mom to watch her?"

"No I wanna do this alone. I'm gonna need to use one of your cars."

"Sure."

"I'll be up there in a few minutes."

Randy quickly started clearing the dishes from the dining room table. He placed them in the dishwasher and started the cycle. Afterward he placed the vase with the carnations in the guest room along with the blanket he and Shanice had laid under the night before. In fifteen minutes, Randy had showered, dressed and freshened the living room with air freshener.

A half hour later, Randy heard Valerie's car pull unto Honey Grove Circle. He opened the door before they had gotten out. Latrease walked up the walkway and onto the porch just as Valerie was closing the door to the car.

"I didn't know you were expecting company." Randy opened the screen door and grabbed the diaper bag from Latrease.

"It's ok I had forgotten they were coming." He walked into the living room behind her and placed the bag on the coffee table.

"Daddy! I missed you." Keyon ran and jumped into Randy's arms giving him a hug.

"Hey squirt, I missed you too."

"You would think you been out of the country or something." Valerie walked in and sat down on the love seat.

"Valerie this is Latrease..." Randy pointed to Latrease, " and this is our daughter Keyana."

"She's adorable."

"Thank you." Latrease said.

"I knew that was my sister!" Keyon got down out of his fathers arm and rushed over beside Latrease to look at the baby.

"Yes, Keyon, she is your sister." Randy said and sat down next to Latrease.

"Can you explain why the two of you felt it necessary to keep this from us?" Valerie took her hat off her head and placed it in her lap. She was wearing a denim dress, red pumps, the hat was out of place. Her hair was braided.

Randy tried to avoid eye contact. He knew from experience that no matter what he said she would have something to say back to create an argument. So less was better.

"Latrease was suffering from amnesia. She didn't remember..."

"I couldn't remember him or the relationship we had. He couldn't tell me." Latrease cut him off.

"Ok, well my problem is that I had to find out all of this through a *five year old*." Valerie gave Randy a sharp stare.

"I don't have a problem with you, Latrease. I just don't like the way things went down." Valerie took a deep breath and continued, " Now since y'all had your baby, Randy hasn't seen my son. Is this gonna be a problem, do I need to have your parental rights removed?"

"Valerie come on, you know I been working my butt off. I received the letter from your lawyer about adjusting the child support, are you serious?"

"Yes Randy you need to spend more time with your son. Anybody can write a check. He's about to start school soon." Valerie said in a matter of fact way.

"Yes I know that, Valerie. I will have my lawyer get in touch with yours and we can make some arrangements and get a legal visitation chart set up. Ok?"

"Why is it that we can't discuss these things without having to involve those white folks. I mean, we should be able to come to an agreement without all the extra mess." Valerie exhaled.

Keyon ran into the guestroom and came back with a toy truck. He then started pushing it around the floor.

Latrease handed the baby to Randy.

"I would love to stay and visit with the two of you but I have an urgent matter to tend to." she said to Valerie and then looked at Randy.

"Are you sure you don't want me to go with you?"

"Go *with* her? Randy we are in the middle of a serious conversation about our child and you are ready to brush us off to run after this little floozy..." Valerie raised her voice.

"I am so tired of you treating our child this way Randy." she continued.

"Look Valerie, I don't have anything to do with your custody issues. You have no right calling me names. You want somebody to respect you, yet you're being rude."

"Calm down ladies, please don't do this in front of the kids." Randy stood up, spread a blanket on the couch and laid the baby on it."

"I apologize, Latrease, you are right, this *is* between me and Randy. I understand if you need to leave." Valerie stood up and offered her hand out to Latrease.

"Truce?"

"Sure." Latrease responded and turned to Randy, "I need your keys."

Randy grabbed the keys to the Lexus off the counter in the kitchen. He felt sick knowing he was sending her out on an unreachable mission. He knew very well where Shanice was; and hoped she'd stay there.

"I put three bottles in the bag. You need to put them in the fridge. There's diapers, wipes, a few blankets and an extra change of clothes. If you need anything else you can get them from my room, you still have your key right?"

"Yes, of course."

"Ok. I will call in a few hours to check on her." Latrease put her handbag on her shoulder.

"Ok, do you know where you are going? What if I need to reach you?" Randy avoided her eyes.

"Well I'm gonna go by my aunts' and see if she has seen her."

"You have an aunt in Atlanta?"

"No, she stays in Albany." Latrease replied.

"Oh, are you sure you don't wanna wait, I can come with you after Valerie leaves." Randy hated the idea of Latrease driving two and a half hours to her hometown for nothing.

"No you two need to work some things out. I will be fine."

She kissed him on the cheek and walked out the door.

Latrease swiped the card again then entered her pin number into the automated teller machine. "What the heck?" she mumbled after reading the screen.

"Insufficient funds? What is wrong with this thing?"

She got back in the car and drove a few more miles down the interstate. She turned off at the next exit and pulled into a Shell Gas Station.

"Does your atm work?" She asked the teenager behind the counter.

"Yes it's right over there."

"Thank you." Latrease walked over to the machine and slid her card in the slot. She punched in her pin number and requested to withdraw three hundred dollars from her savings account. The transaction was declined due to insufficient funds.

"What is going on?" she thought, while attempting to withdraw a smaller amount. After getting the same result she then requested a balance inquiry. She then pulled the ticket out of the machine.

"What the..." Latrease stared at the slip in her hand.

"Twenty dollars." she read it again.

Latrease felt a funny feeling in the pit of her stomach. The last time she'd checked the balance of her savings account was when she and her sister had had lunch with Shemeka. At that time her account had at well over fifteen thousand dollars in it.

Latrease left the store and headed back to Atlanta. She was only forty miles or so out of the city so she figured it was smarter to just turn around. All she could think about was finding Shanice.

"That trifling heffer!"

Latrease put in a TLC CD and skipped through till she got to the song that was on her mind. She sang along to the words of *Case of the fake people*.

She knew without a doubt that her twin sister had taken her money. It was the only thing that made sense. She couldn't help but be angry with herself. She should have seen it coming. This was the sort of thing Shanice was known for. She should have known that her sister wasn't just sticking around to 'help'. Something in her wanted to believe that her sister had changed. She wanted to believe that with everything they'd been through, Shanice would have really wanted to be a sister to her.

Latrease sang along to the song. She thought about how her sister had promised they'd celebrate their twenty second birthday together in March. How could she do this to her? Latrease felt her eyes fill with tears.

An hour later, Latrease was pulling into Honey Grove Circle, she noticed Valerie's car was still parked in front of Randy's house. She decided to go home and come back for the baby later. She parked the car in the garage, and walked around the side of the house, through the garden to the guesthouse.

She pulled her bank information out of her purse and sat at the kitchen table with the cordless phone. She then called her bank. After talking to the branch manager she found out that her sister had physically come into the bank two days prior and withdrew the money. She kept telling herself that it would all be fine. She then called the credit union where the remainder money was from her parents life insurance. It was all but gone too. Shanice had stolen altogether twenty five thousand dollars between the two accounts. Something just didn't seem right. Latrease checked her purse. Everything was in its right place including her drivers license. She needed to talk to someone so she called Bertha.

"Hey girl, is everything alright?" Bertha asked.

"No. Bertha, I'm about to go crazy." Latrease's hand trembled as she held the phone to her ear.

"Calm down it will be alright. She's just letting the boy visit his dad. It's not the end of the world."

"Bertha, what are you talking about?" Latrease asked.

"I saw that witch Valerie's car parked in front of Randy's this afternoon. I know it's hard not knowing what's going on in there, heck if I was you I would just go up there. What she gonna do tell you to leave?"

"I'm not worried about Valerie. I already saw her today." Latrease responded.

"Well what's the matter then, hon?" she asked.

"My sister is missing." Latrease replied.

"Missing?"

"Yes, she is gone."

"I just saw her yesterday, we were talking about going to Vegas for y'alls birthday. Why do you think she's missing, though, she might have just went out with a guy or something?"

"Because she didn't tell me she was leaving with any guy and..."

"I'll be there in about twenty minutes ok?"

"Ok."

Latrease paced the living room floor while waiting for Bertha to get there. She looked in the room her sister had been sleeping in again. She noticed something she hadn't seen in there earlier. There was something sticking out from under the pillow on the bed. Latrease lifted the pillow and picked up the yellow envelope.

She sat down, took a deep breath, then opened it. There was a letter.

My dearest Latrease,
By now you're probably saying to yourself, "I can't believe how someone can do this to me. Especially my own twin" yada yada. You know something, Latrease, I am so tired of that label. Twin. What the heck does it insinuate anyway? Just because we look alike doesn't mean we are alike, right? I mean we have our own personalities. Our own hopes, dreams, and talents.
Do you know how annoying it was growing up being labelled a twin, for me not you? It was great for you! Not only did people not take the time to learn my name but they expected things out of me. You know how everybody in the family expected me to be a good singer, dancer, actress like you?
You know what's even worse? Being labelled the "bad twin". I hate it. I've always hated it. Just because I couldn't sing and win ten thousand dollars at Star Search doesn't make you better than me. Mama and daddy treated you like you were gold. They encouraged you. They went to all your stupid performances and shows. They acted like you were their ticket to riches. They treated me like I was nobody. I wanted to do things too. They never even bothered to know what I liked.

Their obsession with you and all your talents is what caused them their lives. Yeah I was driving the car but had they taken my advice and simply missed that play they would still be here today. But no, despite daddy telling mom the tires need replacing, despite them both being tired from working all day at the restaurant they were still determined to go. Why? Because your nagging annoying butt wouldn't stop calling making them feel bad about missing your stupid opening night. Then I got sucked into the mix and had to drive them.

You know something sister dearest, I will never forgive you for putting that pressure on them.

Now I know you are probably wondering what any of this has to do with, well, you know. Let me see how to put this simple. I have dreams and goals too. I wanna start my own business and I needed the money. I thought you would have at least gave me half of the insurance money but you didn't. So I took it.

Don't even think of coming after me for it either. I happened to stumble across a certain shoe box with a certain diary in it, that was in the shed. It contained a certain diary that clearly tells how you are so much like me it's funny. Interesting, Randy must really love you to not have went through your things, all that time.

I know all about your little plan to trap Randy. That's right, I read all about how you got accepted into Julliard and didn't go because you were afraid if you left Randy would forget your butt. I read all about your little issue with not taking your birth control pills right around the time you were ovulating. I know you know where this is going right?

So now sister deary, when you decide to judge me, ask yourself how much alike we truly are. Don't worry, your secret's safe with me. Oh you'll be fine, you got a rich doctor as a baby daddy who is gonna take care of you for the rest of your life. You will be alright.

Shanice

Latrease folded the letter and put it in her pocket. Tears burned her cheeks as she sat on the bed and cried. It was the longest overdue cry she'd ever held in. A few minutes later she heard a knock at the door.

"Calm down Latrease, we will find her." Bertha hugged Latrease and patted her back.

"It's ok. I know where she's at." Latrease lied.

"Oh ok, well that's good. She's ok, right?"

"Yes. She went back to Albany with my aunt. She's ok." Latrease hated lying but it was the only thing she could think of.

"Where's my sweet niece? Is she sleeping?"

"She's up there with Randy. He was watching her for me..."

"What do you mean, 'watching her for you?' He *is* her father he should be spending time with her just as much as you. Latrease, don't be taking care of that baby all by yourself. Make him help you." Bertha sat down on the couch and crossed her legs.

"I set Bernard straight while we were at the hospital the same day Calvin and Kevin was born. No-sir-ree, I was not bout to be taking care of them babies by myself."

Latrease adjusted the thermostat. "Yeah, I know. He comes back here and visits with her everyday after he gets off for about an hour or so. He's so busy with work and the gym." Latrease sighed.

"Yeah, but you didn't make that baby by yourself. He has to *make* time for her. That's his baby just as much as yours." Bertha was getting edgy. Latrease could tell from her tone.

"Ooh let me show you the new clothes Randy bought the baby." Latrease ran into the other room and started grabbing the clothes from the closet.

Bertha smiled and followed her shaking her head. "You new mothers better stop letting these men get over on you."

"How is she?" Randy sat in the chair across from Dr. Jefferson. The slender gray haired elder man laid the ink pen on the desk.

"She seems fine. She doesn't want to be continue treatment and frankly I believe she will be ok. She has her memory back and that's what matters most." Dr. Jefferson replied.

"Yeah, but it's only been a week, you think that's enough time to have fully evaluated her?"

"She doesn't want treatment. There's nothing more I can do for her unless she voluntarily asks for it. You know that Dr. Jackson."

"Yes, I know. Thank you for your time. I'm glad she at least came these two weeks."

"Yes, we accomplished a lot in those nine sessions. I think she is doing great for having dealt with AMD twice. If there's anything else I can do for you, don't hesitate to call my office."

Randy shook Dr. Jefferson's hand and left the office. He felt good knowing Latrease was doing ok. It had been a week since Shanice left. Randy was still jumpy about the whole situation. No matter how much he tried to forget it, he just couldn't get that night completely out of his head. How could that woman be so devious? He continued asking himself.

On the way home Randy stopped at Lenox Square Mall and went to the jewelry store to pick up the ring.

"So when are you gonna ask her?" The brunette behind the counter asked.

"Well I have reservations for dinner at The Sun Dial."

"Oh nice, that's the restaurant on top of that building right?" The lady nodded in approval.

"Yes, that's where I'm gonna ask her." Randy replied.

"Sounds good. I've never been there before, but my sister's husband took her there for their anniversary and oh man, she said it was nice up there. I'll be routing for you." The lady winked.

After leaving the mall he made a stop at the florist shop. He purchased a bouquet of pink roses and a vase. From there he went to the cleaners to pick up his suit.

A few hours later, after shaving, showering and getting dressed, Randy was on his way through the garden to meet Latrease.

Randy knocked on the door to the guesthouse.

"Just a minute." he heard her sweet voice and felt a tingle in his spine.

When she opened the door, Randy's heart skipped a beat. She was gorgeous. Her hair was up in a french roll with a few curls sprinkled along her face. She was wearing little makeup but her face was glowing. Randy recognized the earrings and necklace she was wearing. He had given them to her on her birthday when she turned twenty one.

She was wearing an aqua colored dress that was not only sexy but laid perfectly over her body. She was wearing black pumps, and the ankle bracelet he had given her for Christmas.

"You are so beautiful, Latrease." Randy held her hand up to his lips and kissed it gently.

"Thank you. You are handsome as usual." She replied.

Latrease took the flowers and sat them on the dining room table.

"Thank you, they are beautiful."

"You are so welcome. You have all of Keyana's stuff ready?" Randy glanced around the living room. It was filled with boxes and huge bags of things that were from the shed. The guesthouse looked different, better to him.

"Shemeka came and got her already. She will be fine." Latrease grabbed her handbag from the coat rack.

"Oh ok."

"I'm ready when you are."

They held hands as they walked slowly through the garden to the front of the estate. It was a warm night with just enough breeze to make Latrease's curls fizzle. Randy couldn't help admiring Latrease. She was beautiful, adorable, everything he had ever wanted in a woman.

"Hey unk," Calvin ran through the garden and stopped in front of them, "Daddy said to tell you that there was a fight at the gym..."

"Oh my." Latrease sighed.

"Is everything ok?" Randy asked.

"Yeah, but I think Fred got arrested." Calvin panted.

"Randy, we can reschedule our date if you need to go..." Latrease turned and looked Randy in the eyes.

"Oh no. Bernard can handle this. Tell him to take care of it, Cal, you and your brother go down there and help out."

"But we don't have a way to get there." The teen replied.

"Here take the other car." Randy took the key off the key-chain and handed it to Calvin.

"Take care of my car and don't speed."

Randy wasn't going to let this interfere with his plans for the night. He'd never let his nephews drive his car, but it was the only way to handle the situation.

"Thanks unk. I will be extra careful with your car. Which one you letting me drive?"

"Look at the key." Randy replied.

"Oh duh." Calvin smiled.

"Hey Miss Trease, you look nice tonight, where you and my uncle going?"

"I don't know Calvin. He hasn't told me yet." Latrease looked up in Randy's eyes.

"Unk, why y'all dressed up?" the teen asked.

"That's for me to know and you to..." The boy nodded.

"Find out right?"

"Exactly. See you later Calv."

"Aight unk." Calvin gave his uncle some dap and headed back to his house.

The ride to the restaurant was refreshing. Latrease was in a great mood. She was feeling beautiful and sexy. It had been four weeks since she gave birth to Keyana, and this was the first time she'd really felt like herself again.

She was happy that Randy was spending more time with her and the baby. Every morning before he went to work he stopped in to feed the baby and change her. At night he would read her a story and assist with giving her a bath. Keyana had grown so much in those four weeks.

Keyana payed more attention to Latrease now and whenever she would move, Keyana's eyes followed. Whenever Latrease stuck her tongue out Keyana copied. She wasn't sure if it was coincidental or not. She'd even noticed that whenever she put her finger in Keyana's hand, she would grasp it as if holding it. Keyana responded whenever she heard Randy's voice. It was like she knew that he was her daddy.

She even responded to Bertha. She never cried when Bertha held her. She loved to lay on Bertha's chest, and fall asleep.

Randy had started getting Keyon more often. Latrease was happy about that. Keyon adored the baby. He would sit next to Latrease and hold the bottle in Keyana's mouth when she needed feeding. He would hold the diaper and place it in the trash can when Latrease changed the baby. Latrease enjoyed spending time with Keyon. Everytime he would come over, he'd ask her to sing his favorite song, *Twinkle, Twinkle Little Star*. He would often sing along.

Latrease gazed out of the window of the Mercedes Benz. The city was amazing. The buildings stood tall, bold, and lit up the sky. Randy pulled into a parking garage at what looked like the Westin Peachtree Plaza, and collected the ticket at the booth. Latrease wondered where they were going.

Randy was looking like a chocolate Easter bunny that Latrease wanted to rip into. He was wearing that cologne she loved smelling. His hair was cut and face was freshly shaven. Latrease could smell the aftershave. "Mmmm." she mumbled to herself.

After parking the car, Randy opened the door for Latrease. He kissed her hand and escorted her to the elevator. After a three minute elevator ride to the top of the skyscraper Latrease opened her eyes and smiled.

The restaurant was beautiful. The hostess greeted them and escorted them to their table.

"Did you know that the Western Peachtree Plaza is the tallest hotel in the western hemisphere?"

Latrease smiled. "Nope."

"Neither did I, until when I called to make reservations." Randy giggled.

"This place is beautiful, Randy." Latrease admired the wonderfully decorated atmosphere. The view was phenomenal. There was a band that played soft music, and a bar fully stocked bar.

The waitress greeted them with a smile.

"Hi. My name is Miss Ann, and I will be your waitress tonight. What can I get the two of you to drink?"

Latrease admired the waitress. She was the only black waitress in the restaurant. She was pretty, with big brown eyes and a nice smile.

"Latrease would you like a bottle of champagne?" Randy looked up from the menu and gazed at Latrease.

"I've never had champagne before, does it taste anything like the wine we had at the other restaurant?" She held her head down a bit embarrassed that she hadn't had more experience with alcohol.

"It's good. I think you will like it." the waitress told her.

"Ok, but maybe a small bottle; just in case I don't."

"We'll take a bottle of Dom Pérignon." Randy told the waitress.

"Oh my, Randy, that champagne is almost three hundred dollars. I think that's a bit expensive."

"It's fine. Relax babe."

The waitress left and returned with the bottle on ice and two glasses.

"Would you like to order appetizers?" she asked.

"No. Every time I eat appetizers I get full and can't eat my meal." Latrease explained.

The waitress giggled. "How about you sir?"

"No, I think I am ready to order. I'll have the herb roasted lamb-chops, minus the egg plant."

"Ok. Are you ready to order as well ma'am?" the waitress looked up at Latrease.

"Yes, I'll have the boursin encrusted beef filet. Oh, and I'll take the cheesecake for desert." Latrease closed the menu and handed it back to the waitress.

After eating her meal, she excused herself from the table and went to the ladies room. When she came back her desert was sitting on the table.

"Mmmm this is good" Latrease smiled in a teasing way she held up her fork. "You want some of this sweet stuff?"

"Yes, I sure do, but I don't think you can fit it all on that tiny plate."

Latrease smiled.

Randy watched attentively as Latrease finished the last bit of her cheesecake, then frowned in disappointment.

"What's the matter, did you want some for real?"

"No, what was that waitresses name again?" Randy waved his hand up in the air to get the woman's attention.

"Umm, I think it was Annie, ...no Ann." Latrease swallowed.

The woman placed the plates on the table next to them and then walked over to Randy.

"How may I help you?"

"There's a problem with the desert." The waitress glanced at the table with a blank look on her face.

"What's the problem?" the waitress looked at Latrease then back at Randy.

"It was too cold. She could barely eat it."

"I'm sorry, sir, would you like me to get her another piece?"

"No I don't. I don't feel like I should have to pay for this meal."

"Well I will have to talk to the manager about that. I will be right back."

"Ann there was nothing..."

"Latrease let her do her job." Randy cut her off.

Latrease was annoyed. Why was Randy giving that poor waitress such a hard time? She didn't understand it at all. There was nothing wrong with her desert, in fact it was actually the best cheesecake she'd ever eaten. Randy was being a total jerk.

"What the heck is wrong with you, Randy?" Latrease snapped.

"If the food is not right I should not have to pay for it. Plain and simple. As a matter of fact I'm gonna go find that manager myself."

Randy got up and walked away from the table. Latrease felt blood rush to her face. She was beyond embarrassed. She'd never seen Randy act this way before. He was making a complete fool of himself. And her. What was his problem?

A few seconds later, the singer from the band came over to the table. He was holding a microphone in his hand.

"Are you Latrease Wilson?" The man with the microphone asked.

"Yes, I am."

"I need you to come with me." the man held his hand out to assist her.

"Why? What's going on? Look I don't have a problem with the food. I don't know what my date's problem is. I'm sorry he..."

"I need you to come with me Miss Wilson."

Latrease followed the man to the stage where she saw Randy walk over to her and kneel down on one knee.

"Latrease I love you so much. The last seven months I realized how much I need you in my life. You make me better. Latrease Renee Wilson, will you marry me?"

Latrease felt butterflies in her stomach. Her cheeks were flushed and she was shivering.

"Yes, Randy, Yes!" Randy held her hand in his and slid the ring onto her finger. He stood up and gave her a kiss.

The band started playing the tune of Jesse Powells song titled, *You*. Latrease loved this song. The guy with the microphone started singing the words. Latrease and Randy danced, holding each other.

The next few days went by rather fast for Randy. He and Latrease had decided to have a small wedding in the field next to Shemeka's house. Randy's mom and Shemeka had self appointed themselves to do the planning, they insisted.

The date was set for May fourteenth, the day after Latreases spa extravaganza. That gave them a week and a half to get everything planned and paid for. Randy wasn't that thrilled with having it so soon but Latrease wanted to be married before they were intimate again.

Randy couldn't help but feel a cringe in his stomach whenever someone mentioned Shanice. When they were at the engagement dinner and his mother asked if Shanice would be the maid of honor Randy almost blurted out, *no*, but Latrease beat him to it. He didn't understand why but it seemed Latrease had no interest in her sister ever coming back. Not that he wanted her to either. Randy noticed that every time someone brought up Shanice, Latrease changed the subject. He wondered, but wouldn't dare ask.

Randy parked the Lexus in front of Valerie's house and walked up the steps to knock on the door.

"You came to pick up your boy?" Valerie's husband walked out onto the porch wearing a muscle shirt and jean shorts.

"Yes, is he ready?" Randy replied.

"I don't know. Let me see." The guy went back into the house and closed the screen door as if to let Randy know he wasn't welcome inside. Randy had never had a problem with Valerie's husband before, but ever since they'd made agreement on visitation, He had seemed moody when Randy came around.

"He'll be out there in a minute." The guy came back and then closed the door along with the wooden door as well.

Randy walked down the steps and waited for his son by the car. He was not in the mood for a confrontation, he just wanted to get Keyon.

"Hey daddy." The boy dragged his suitcase down the steps. Randy rushed over and picked him up.

"Hi Squirt. What you been up to?"

The boy laughed as Randy tickled him under the arm.

"Nothing, playing."

Randy put the suitcase in the car and strapped the boy in the seat.

"Where Miss Treasie?" Keyon asked.

"She's at home with the baby." Randy answered, starting the ignition.

"I can't wait to see Keyana, I got her something."

Keyon pulled a toy car from his pocket.

"Wow man, that's too small for Keyana, but how about I take you to the toy store and you can get her something else."

"Ooh, daddy, can I get me something too?"

"Yes, of course."

A few hours later, Randy was pulling into Honey Grove Circle. He parked the car in the garage and opened the door for his son, who had fallen asleep. Randy laid the boy in the guestroom then went into the kitchen to get something to drink. When he went to put the glass in the sink he noticed the light blinking on the answering machine.

He pushed the button to play the messages.

Heyyyyy brutha-in-law what you wearing tonight. beep

Heyyyyyy brutha-in-law how's my sister doing? beep

Heyyyyyy brutha-in-law call me on this number. beep

Hey brutha-in-law I miss you. Beep

Randy paced the kitchen floor. What was her problem! Why was she doing this? What if Latrease had been there and heard this? Randy tried not to let it get him upset. The phone rang.

"Hello."

"Heyyyyyyyy brutha-in-law, for a minute there I thought you were screening my calls. Then I thought, now why would he want to do that? Especially since we have so much chemistry, now don't we?"

Randy sat down at the table.

"Shanice, why are you calling me?"

"I was bored and I was missing you, don't you miss me brutha-in-law?" she replied.

"Well, I'm sure you have someone else you can call when you get bored."

"Yeah, but they're no fun. I like to play. Don't you like playing with me, Randy?"

"No. I don't want you calling my house anymore. Do you understand?" Randy grabbed a pen and pad from the drawer by the sink.

"But I need..."

Shanice, I don't know what kind of game you are playing but it stops here. I tried to be nice to you, you took advantage of that and you tricked me."

"Is that what you call it? Well I don't think that's what it will look like to Treasie, by the way how is my sister and that adorable little baby of yours?" Randy squeezed the phone cord in his hand.

"What do you want, Shanice?" Randy asked.

"Well dang, you ain't gonna ask me how I'm doing or nothing?" she sassed.

"No. what is it that you want from me?"

"I need to come home. I'm broke. I lost all the money gambling."

"You gambled away twenty five thousand dollars in one week?" Randy raised his tone.

"No I lost the whole fifty grand." she sighed.

"What fifty grand? I only gave you twenty five."

"Yeah well you ain't the only one with secrets. Tell my sister I'm on my way. I need you to pick me up at the airport at seven tonight. Oh and don't bring anybody with you."

"Shanice, I am not..."

Randy heard the dial-tone on the other end of the phone. "What a big mess", he thought.

Randy dialed his mothers number. "Hey mom."

"Hey Bernard."

"Mom, this is Randy."

"Oh, I'm sorry, chile, y'all sound alike sometimes. What's going on?" she asked.

"Nothing, I just wanted to see if you can watch Keyon later? I have some errands to run."

"Depends on how late, I'm supposed to go with the girls to get sized for dresses. I'm so excited about this wedding. I'm proud of you, Randy, you got yourself a good girl."

"Yeah, I know mom. I need to leave around six this evening."

"Oh that's fine, we should be back way before then."

"Thanks a million, I'll bring him over then."

"Where my grandson at now? I got some cookies in the jar on the table that Kevin brought over last night."

"He's sleeping. Just save them for when I bring him."

"Ok then, see you later."

"Alright, bye mom."

"How long will it take for you to make the adjustments?" Latrease bit her nail.

"It can be ready in two days. I know you need them soon but I have to order the others, they will get here Friday and then I have to make a few alterations."

Latrease sighed.

" Don't worry, all of the dresses will be ready before the wedding, next Saturday." The lady continued.

"Ok, as long as I'm not walking down the aisle in a sheet, then that's fine with me." Latrease started gathering her things.

"You are gonna be the most beautiful bride since, I got married in back in 1968." Randy's mom teased.

"Eh unm" Bertha cleared her throat.

"Oh dang I forgot all about you Bertha, but you know justice of the peace marriages don't count."

"Justice of the whuh?" Latrease asked.

"Peace." Bertha replied. "Me and Bernard couldn't afford a wedding so we got married at the courthouse. You know Bernard didn't have all that money like Randy does. He actually had to work for his."

"Bertha don't start that, you know darn well Bernard wasn't trying to work back then. That's why their dad left that gym to Randy in the first place."

"Yeah, Bernard was running round acting like a chicken with his head cut off." Shemeka added.

"Stop, instigating." Bertha shot her a hard glance.

"I'm not instigating, heck, they both my brothers, I'm just telling it like it I-S is." Shemeka shrugged her shoulders up.

"Ladies please don't argue, I hate it when sisters are bitter at each other." Latrease waved her hand in the air to get their attention.

"Well we're not actually sisters, but I get what you're saying." Shemeka replied.

"Speaking of sisters, is Shanice coming to the wedding?" Bertha asked and handed her dress to the woman.

"No."

"Why not..." Bertha raised her brow, "If I had a twin sister she would definitely be at my wedding. She would be my maid of honor."

"She's busy. She has to take care of our aunt. I told you this already Bertha." Latrease was fidgety at the subject of her sister. She didn't want her anywhere near her wedding. She didn't want her anywhere near Randy.

"Yeah, I know but she could bring your aunt with her. I mean, you're only gonna have this nice wedding once." Bertha replied.

"I know, I'll call her and see." Latrease lied. She had no intention of calling her sister. She needed to get Bertha to stop pestering her about it so she said what she had to.

"Well ladies would you like lunch, while we're out? It's my treat." Randy's mom asked.

"Sure." Shemeka replied.

"Yes, I would love to." Bertha agreed.

"How about you, Treasie?"

"I don't know, I think I need to get back to the baby."

"Treasie," Bertha put her hand on her hip, "what did I tell you about that? He's her father. He needs to spend time with her just like you. He's fine, trust me."

"I guess." Latrease shrugged her shoulders.

A few minutes later the four were at the China Wok Buffet. Latrease grabbed an empty plate and walked around the buffet adding items on it. She glanced over at Randy's mother, who had been smiling at her ever since the engagement dinner.

Latrease wondered if her soon to be mother-in-law would still smile if she knew what Latrease had done. She knew the answer, she had to keep her sister away. She thought about the last time she'd seen her. Shanice had been so kind, so caring. What would make her run off with her money like that?

Latrease placed the plate on the table and sat in the empty seat.

"Girl I tried to wait on you, but you looked like you were up there daydreaming. You know me I loves to eat." Bertha said holding a piece of chicken up to her mouth.

"It's ok, there was so many choices."

"Awe Latrease is just nervous, you got those wedding bell jitters. Don't you?" Shemeka opened her napkin and spread it over her lap.

"I guess. A little." Latrease smiled and started eating.

"I knew you were the one. Remember when I first met you, I said, y'all were getting married, didn't I?" Shemeka asked.

"Yeah, but..."

"*But* nothing, I *know* my brother. Haha."

The ladies ate and chatted. Latrease enjoyed their company. It was refreshing to be out with a group of women that wanted only good things for her. They'd been so supportive ever since she first moved into the guesthouse. They never treated her like an outcast.

When the ladies got back to Honey Grove Circle the first thing Latrease noticed was that Randy was out in the yard playing catch with Keyon. She instantly wondered where the baby was.

"I'm sure she's alright." Bertha patted her hand.

"How did you..."

"I'm a mother." Bertha smiled.

Shemeka parked the car and the ladies said their goodbyes. Latrease walked over to the yard.

"Miss Treasie!" Keyon ran and hugged her.

"Hi big boy. Whatcha doing out here?" she asked putting the boy back down.

"Daddy is showing me how to catch."

" I see."

Randy walked over to Latrease and kissed her on the forehead.

"Hey babe. How was the fitting?"

"It was nice, my dress is beautiful." she replied.

"I bet it is. I can't wait to see my baby in her dress." Randy winked.

"Yeah, well you have to wait, at least till the wedding." she smiled.

"Ok, ok, I can wait and what a wonderful time we are gonna have after the wedding."

"Can I at least have a hint where we're going."

"Nope, sorry." He replied.

"Ok, I won't keep asking, unless you're gonna tell me?" she smiled.

"Where's Keyana?" Latrease casually asked even though it was the first thing she wanted to ask since she got out of the car.

"She's in the house." Randy tossed the ball to Keyon. "She is sleeping. Kevin is in there with her."

"Oh, ok. Well I'm gonna check on her." Before he could say anything Latrease was up the steps and in the house.

As soon as she got in, the phone rang.

"What up." Kevin picked up the phone.

Latrease waved and walked past him. The baby was in the bassinet in the living room. She was still asleep. Latrease pulled the thin blanket over the baby, then started gathering her bottles from the fridge.

Randy and Keyon, walked into the house.

"Ok, lil man, I'ma get you some stuff together so you can go over grandma's for a lil bit." Randy told the boy.

"Do I have to?" Keyon pouted.

Kevin walked into the living room.

"Unk, Shanice say she ready."

Randy looked at the teen and shook his head.

"Alright, I need you to walk Keyon over to mamas." Randy grabbed Keyons suitcase and handed it to Kevin.

"Tell her he needs a bath, he's been outdoors all day."

"Randy, was that my sister?" Latrease asked.

"Yes, she's at the airport. I'mma go scoop her up and be right back love." Randy kissed her on the cheek.

"Scoop her up and take her where?" Latrease bit her lower lip.

"Your place." He replied.

"I don't want her at my..."

"Unk, why she at the airport? Ain't Albany just a few minutes down the highway?" Kevin interrupted her.

"Yeah, well that's where she needs me to pick her up from." Randy told him.

"Well that's good, now she can be in the wedding." Kevin replied.

"NO!" Latrease snapped.

Randy gave her a confused stare.

"I mean, I'm sure she has to get back to my aunt. She probably just came for the rest of her things. Matter of fact, Randy, I'll ride with you. I already have her stuff packed up. I can run grab it and throw it all in the car."

The teenager grabbed the boy by the hand and started walking towards the door.

"Come on, Keyon, lets get outta here, too much grown up talk going on for our young ears."

"Latrease, it's getting late. I can handle it. How about you just stay here. Get comfortable and I will be right back. Ok, darling?" Randy motioned for her to sit down on the couch.

Latrease sat back on the couch and watched Randy leave. Her brain was racing a million miles a minute. All she could think of was what her sister was gonna say to Randy in that half an hour car ride.

Randy placed the parking ticket on the dashboard and parked the car. He hated coming to Hartsfield International Airport, the biggest airport in the states, because it was so easy to get lost. He even hated it more since he was there to pick up Shanice.

It didn't take long for Randy to spot her. She was in the baggage claim area bent over the conveyor belt wearing a skirt that was too short, that revealed thongs that were too small. He wasn't trying to look but it was the first thing he saw.

All of the men were flocked around her. Pretending to help but at the same time staring up her skirt. She seemed to enjoy the attention. Smiling and licking her lips in a seductress way.

"Heyyyyy brutha-in-law." Shanice walked over and gave Randy a sloppy kiss on the cheek that he quickly wiped off.

"Are you ready?" Randy avoided eye contact.

"As ready as I'll ever be." she replied and handed him two suitcases.

"So, what are your plans?"

"I was thinking I can just crash at your place and find a job somewhere maybe work at your gym, Latrease told me she made good money there."

"No! You can not! Look Shanice, I did what you asked me. I gave you the money even though you had a messed up way of getting it out of me. If you had come to me and said, 'Randy I want to do something with my life, I need some help financially'...I would have had no problem helping and encouraging you. What you pulled that night was cruel and deceptive." Randy put the luggage in the trunk. Then clicked the key remote to unlock the door.

"You can stay in my guesthouse for three months, no longer than that. Then, I want you gone."

"Latrease won't want me...What if I don't find anywhere..."

"That's not my problem."

The drive home was long. Randy avoided speeding because there seemed to be state patrolmen at every couple of miles down the highway. Shanice didn't say much. She just sat there playing with her curls, and picking the nail polish from her nails.

"Hows Keyana?"

"She's good."

"I bet she misses me." Shanice stretched the arm strap from the seatbelt pulling it out from her body and then let it go.

"I don't know about that but I'm sure she will remember you when she sees you."

When they arrived at the house Randy carried the luggage to the guesthouse and unlocked the door.

"Latrease, is at my house. She will be here soon. We're good, right?" Randy asked giving her eye contact for the first time since he'd picked her up.

"Yeah, we good brutha-in-law, but I'm gonna need a ride to go job hunting. You gonna have to let me use one of your cars." She started swinging her arms.

"Yeah, I will let you use the Lexus while you look for a job and to get back and forth to that job. Not for going out partying and all that mess you like to do."

"Ok, sounds like a deal." Shanice told him.

Randy walked slowly through the garden. He was sure Latrease would still be awake since it wasn't late. He was exhausted, he felt depleted. It was the first time since he proposed that he was afraid. He wished he could turn back the hands of time. He wish he'd been able to differentiate between the two of them. He wondered what it would be like to be married to a twin, not only a twin, but one with a vindictive sister like Shanice.

Just as Randy was exiting the garden he saw someone over by the rose bushes. What was she doing out there he wondered.

"Hey babe, I just walked your sister to the house." She didn't budge.

"Latrease, hon what are you doing out here?" She continued to look out in space.

Randy walked over and tapped her on the shoulder. "Latrease, are you ok?"

"I can't do this." She replied frantically.

"Do what honey, what's the matter?" Randy asked.

"I can't marry you. I'm a horrible person." she started crying.

"Latrease, honey, what's wrong?" Randy knelt down and rubbed her back.

"How can you marry someone you can't trust?" She looked him in the eyes.

"Latrease, I love you. Not anyone else. You are the one for me." Randy grabbed her hand and helped her up.

"We are doing the right thing, baby."

"Yeah, well why do I feel the way I do? I feel so..."

Randy leaned in and kissed her on the eyelid. He then kissed her on her lips. He wrapped his arms around her waste and continued kissing her.

Before long they were lying on the grass, kissing and caressing each other. Randy kissed her lips, her ears, her neck. He gazed upon her breasts and coupled them in his hands. He then unbuttoned the first three buttons of her blouse as he continued kissing her body. Latrease slid her panties down under her skirt, inviting him to pleasure her.

"Randy Jackson, I want to be your wife." Latrease whispered in his ear.

"I know baby."

Randy slid his erection into her hot wet center.

"Mmm baby you feel so good." he mumbled.

She wrapped her legs around his waist and kissed his neck. Sucking it hard and fast. Randy loved every bit of it. With each thrust she moaned in ecstasy.

That night they made love right there in the garden under the stars.

Latrease woke up to breakfast in bed. Randy prompted her to sit up then slid the tray up to her. There were three plates on the tray that included; eggs, hashbrowns, grits, pancakes, bacon, sausage, and toast.

"Look familiar?" Randy smiled and placed a cup of orange juice on the tray.

"Yeah, you got jokes." She replied then added, "But I like your kinda humor."

"Well enjoy your breakfast, I'm gonna go and get Keyon in the tub then get the baby taken care of and fed."

"Wow, Superdad." Latrease said grace and started eating her breakfast. She felt good, relaxed. It had been a long time since she was in Randy's bed. It felt good to be there. As she ate she looked around the room wondering what things she would change about it when she moved in.

The walls were still bare. No pictures, no decorations. She thought about the things she had in the guesthouse that she had added from her old apartment. They wouldn't match Randy's furniture and bed spread. She knew she would probably have to buy some new stuff.

The food was good even though she wasn't able to finish it. Latrease moved the tray and got up and walked into the bathroom. There were candles all over the room. The tub was filled with bubbles and there was a yellow summer dress hanging on the hanger with a pair of black thongs. Latrease immediately recognized them both. They were always kept in the drawer she had at Randys. After they had been seeing each other for about six months she decided to have a drawer to keep a few things in. That dress was one of them.

Latrease pulled the t-shirt over her head and climbed into the bath. It was nice and hot, just the way she liked it. There was soft music playing in the boombox that sat on the shelf. Latrease stretched her body out in the tub and relaxed. It was so peaceful as she closed her eyes and enjoyed the music:

A few minutes later she was dressed and had brushed her hair up in a ponytail. She felt good, her body was in relaxed. The tension she'd been feeling, released. All she had was happy thoughts.

She went into the living room where Randy was giving Keyana a bottle. Keyon was on the floor pushing his toy truck around. He looked up and saw Latrease. His face lit up.

"Miss Treasie!" he ran over and gave her a hug.

"Hi Keyon, whatcha doing?"

"Playing with my truck, waiting on daddy to finish feeding my baby sister so I can hold her." He pointed to the baby then pushed the truck across the floor to the other side of the room.

The doorbell rang. Latrease walked over to it.

"Who is it?" she asked.

"It's me sister deary." Shanice opened the door and barged in.

"You know, you could have at least came and said hi to me last night." Latrease fought her urge to slap her.

"I'm sorry, I was busy with my fiance'." She held her hand out and showed her the ring.

"Oh my, Treasie, it's gorgeous."

"Thank you." she replied and they hugged.

"I am happy for you." Shanice smiled.

Latrease looked at her twin sister and wondered how they could look so much alike but act so different. She knew that her sister's congrats were real. She knew that she wanted the best for her, despite what she had done.

"Are you ok, Niecy?"

"Yeah, fine."

Randy entered the kitchen with the baby in his arms. His smile was replaced by a frown.

"Hi Shanice."

"Whuddup, brutha-in-law," she walked over and gave him a kiss on the cheek.

"How come you didn't tell me you were about to be my real brutha-in-law? I thought we were closer than that."

"It slipped my mind." he answered.

Latrease gave him a hard stare. How could their engagement slip his mind? She wondered. It definitely didn't slip hers. As a matter of fact, every single day since they became engaged Latrease thought about it. She'd been working closely with Randy's mom and sister on every single detail of the wedding. How could he simply forget about it.

Latrease wondered if she was reading too much into it. Randy was a very busy man, juggling his career, the gym, and parenting. He was doing so much it was making her tired from watching.

"Yeah because I thought your sister would have already told you. Everybody knows about this wedding." Randy shot a hard glance at Latrease then handed Shanice the baby.

"Hey auntie baby, you missed me didn't you?" Shanice held the baby up on her shoulder and patted her on the back.

"She is getting big." She looked at Randy. "She has your smile." she added.

"Thanks."

"Well I just came to get the keys I have an interview in forty minutes."

"Interview, you planning on staying?" Latrease raised her brows."

"Yeah, for a while, Randy said I can stay in the guesthouse until I get on my feet. He's such a wonderful man. You got you a good one. Don't ever do anything dishonest to lose him, he's one of a kind." She snickered.

Keyon walked into the kitchen.

"Holy Cow, there are two Miss Treasies" Shanice handed the baby to Latrease.

"Hi big boy and what are you up to today?"

"Um nothing, just playing." Keyon blinked hard then looked up at the ladies again.

"That's my sister, Shanice, we're twins, like your cousins, Calvin and Kevin."

"But they are boys, y'all are girls." Keyon looked at her in a confused way.

"Yes, twins can be girls too."

Shanice leaned down and held her hand out to shake his.

"Hi Keyon."

"Hi. You look a lot like Miss Treasie, but I can tell the difference now."

"Really?" Latrease asked.

"Yep." and with that he walked out of the kitchen. Randy was handing Shanice the keys when she gave him a weird look.

"I guess a person *could* tell us apart if they really wanted to." she said.

The day before the wedding, crept up on Latrease, quickly. She had decided to invite her sister, Bertha and Shemeka, to go along with her on the spa day. She didn't want to be alone. Although she would have preferred to only have Bertha and Shemeka come along, she knew she couldn't leave her sister alone unsupervised. She didn't want to risk her spilling information to Randy or his mother or even Bernard.

Bertha had told her that the only way she would go is if Shanice came too. She didn't trust her around Bernard. She didn't trust any women around him so that was nothing new.

Latrease woke up to a knock at her bedroom door.

"Come in." She sat up in the bed.

"Hey girl. Mama wanted me to come get the baby and bring her up there to the house."

"I thought Randy was watching her today."

"Yeah, well I heard my brother talking about some kinda get together they were planning on having for him tonight." She sat down on the edge of the bed.

"Oh really, like a bachelor party?" Latrease got up and started getting dressed.

"I guess. Don't worry Bernard ain't gonna let anything get out of hand."

"I'm not worried." She smiled.

Shanice walked into the room. "I already packed her stuff up do you want me to go ahead and drop her off at Randys?"

"No I'm taking her to mama's." Shemeka told her.

"Oh ok, I thought Randy was..."

"The plans were changed, he is going out tonight." Latrease explained.

"Are you sure you can trust him around all those strippers? You know how weak he gets under pressure."

"Excuse you?" Shemeka stood up.

"There's a lot of things my brother is, but weak is not one of them."

"Yeah and there's a lot of secrets around here that would suggest otherwise." Shanice rolled her eyes then added, "I'm just sayin."

"What the heck..."

"Ladies calm down, I don't have a problem with Randy having a party. Lets get ready to go, today is all about us being pampered." Latrease grabbed her suitcase, makeup bag, and her wedding dress and carried them all to Shemeka's car.

Shemeka put the baby in the stroller and grabbed the baby's things, then took her to her mothers house.

Shanice didn't move.

"Come on, Niecy, get your things. We're leaving in a few minutes." Latrease pleaded.

"I don't want to go. You go on and have fun with your soon to be sister in laws. I'mma just hang out around here." She snapped.

"Niecy I want you to come with me. Don't act like that. Let's go relax and have fun together."

"I don't want to. I'll see you tomorrow at the wedding. Now, go on, have some fun. I'm ok, I just want to get some rest."

Latrease gave her sister a hug and joined the others in the car.

Randy woke up to the sound of gunfire on the television. "Bernard, what time is it?" he saw his brother out of the corner of his eye.

"You good it's only ten."

"Ten? Why you didn't wake me up?"

"Chill out bro, I ain't gonna let you be late for your own wedding." Bernard replied looking down at his watch.

"Besides, you have all of five hours before the wedding." he continued.

"Yeah and I have to get my hair cut, shave, go pick up our tuxedos, and everything."

"Calm down, Fred already picked up all the tuxedo's. I made an appointment for your hair cut in an hour. Relax, I got you." Bernard picked up a small bottle of whisky and poured some in a shot glass.

"Here man, it'll help you loosen up." Randy drank the liquor and stood up.

"I need to check on those tickets. Fred can I use your phone?" Randy looked around the living room of Fred's apartment. There was so much clutter it was hard to see the furniture. Pizza boxes, beer cans, and chip bags were all over the place.

Randy reminisced on the night before. He, Bernard, Fred and Curt had went to Club Nickys. They'd had a good time but Randy was ready to go when he first got there. Bernard had paid the girls to give him a special lap dance but he declined. Fred stepped up and got the dance. He said he didn't want the money to be wasted.

Randy called the travel agency.

"Hi this is Randy Jackson, I just wanted to confirm my vacation is booked and solid."

"You and your wife will be flying to Jamaica?"

"Yes." Randy replied.

"Everything is good. Your flight leaves out of Hartsfield International Airport at four o'clock tomorrow evening." The lady on the other end assured.

"Ok, thank you."

A few hours later Randy and his brother arrived at Honey Grove Circle. There were cars parked all around the cul de sac and in every garage and driveway. Randy was excited about the wedding, even though he couldn't get that nervous feeling out of the pit of his stomach. He still felt uncomfortable about Shanice being there and more annoyed that she was the maid of honor. Of all titles.

Randy stood behind the flower arrangement and waited for his cue. He watched as the guests were seated. The lawn was decorated beautifully. All of the chairs were white with lavender ribbons that laced around the top. There were yellow and lavender flower arrangements on every aisle. There was a white runner that went down the middle between the brides side of guests and the grooms side.

Randy caught a glimpse of Armentha and her husband and children. They were sitting on the brides side. They were the only ones over there.

The music started playing and Calvin and Kevin passed out programs. Everyone took their seats. Randy hadn't seen Latrease in two days, he missed her and couldn't help but wonder if his soon to be sister in law had said anything to her. He'd tried to avoid her as much as possible over the last few days.

Randy walked down the aisle with his mother who was wearing a beautiful lavender dress. He stood in front of the preacher anxiously waiting to see his soon to be wife. Shemeka marched down with Fred and Bertha marched with Curt.

My Endless Love played through the loud speaker. Bernard and Shanice marched down the aisle. She was wearing a yellow dress. Her hair was straightened and hanging down to the back. Bernards' tux was black and yellow to accent her dress.

Next he saw Fred's daughter walking down the aisle throwing flowers from a basket. Dr. Jefferson walked down the aisle with Latrease. She was gorgeous. Randy's heart fluttered as she walked up and stood in front of him. Her hair was up in a frenchroll and bangs of curls dangled. She was beautiful Randy almost lost his breath.

A few hours later they were dancing at the reception. Everyone was having a good time enjoying themselves. The food was good, Randy had to admit his mom and sister knew how to throw a party.

Randy's mother walked up to the band and grabbed the microphone.

"I would like to make a toast to my son and his beautiful wife, Latrease. May your days be filled with love, respect, honesty and trust. And let no man, or woman come between this beautiful union that God has put together."

"I guess two out of four ain't bad." Shanice yelled from across the room.

"You bout to get on my last nerve." Shemeka shook her head in disbelief.

Randy panicked. Grabbed his sister by the arm. "Meek I think you've had too much to drink."

"*I've* had too much to drink? Are you serious?" She yanked her arm from his grasp. "This chick here been making snarky remarks ever since she got back from her aunts. If you ask me, Latrease, I think she's jealous."

"Jealous? And what exactly do you think I'm jealous of?" Shanice came closer. Bertha walked over and tried to get her to back off.

"Jealous that your sister has a handsome loving man that loves and adores her and a beautiful daughter."

"Why would *I* be jealous of *them*. She ain't nothing to be jealous of."

Latrease rushed over to her sisters side. Randy felt his hands tremble.

"Heck, anybody can trap a baby on somebody."

"What are you talking about, Shanice, your sister didn't even know she was pregnant until after her accident."

Shanice laughed out loud. Randy's mom walked over and pointed at Shanice.

"Young lady, why are you trying to spoil your sisters big day. We have done nothing but be nice to you. She let you stay with her. Why are you saying these hurtful things?"

"Because it's the truth." Shanice turned back and faced Shemeka and Randy.

"Is that what you believe? Well you are as pathetic as I thought. She trapped you. She stopped taking her birth control and got pregnant on purpose."

"Now that is enough! You need to leave this place right now!" Randys mom pointed to the door.

"Tell em Latrease, tell em all about your little plan to get Randy to commit to you. Tell em."

Randy turned and looked his new bride in the eyes.

"Is this true, Latrease?" Shemeka asked.

Latrease dropped to the floor with her face in her hands.

"How could you do that to him?" Shemeka asked.

Randy walked over and tried to grab her hands. Her whole body trembled.

"Is this true."

Latrease was crying a river of tears.

"Answer me, Latrease did you purposely get pregnant to force me to marry you."

"Yes." she sobbed.

"Told ya!" Shanice laughed.

"You know something, that was not your place to tell him that. They are happy, how could you be so cruel?" Bertha rolled her eyes.

"Why not, he needed to know." Shanice snapped.

Bertha handed Latrease a napkin she had picked up off one of the tables so she could wipe her face.

"It's ok, Latrease. I love you. I love our daughter. You are my wife now."

"Yeah plus he has a few skeletons in his closet too." Shanice blurted out.

"I am about to slap this chick." Shemeka started taking off her jewelry.

"Let it go, Meek, we're family now." Randy felt butterflies in his stomach.

"Yeah and everybody here loves everybody, right Randy. I mean isn't that what you told me that night we made out?"

Latrease raised her head up.

"Baby, she is lying."

"No I am not. It happened Treasie. I went over there to talk to him about staying longer. He slipped something in my drink. That's why I left. He gave me twenty five grand to disappear."

"What the heck is going on with you three. Randy, I did not raise you to be doing mess like this." Randy's mom exclaimed.

"Party's over, everybody get out of here." She started directing the crowd to leave.

"You made out with my sister?" Randy could see the shock on her face.

"Yes, no, it's not what you think." Randy stuttered.

"We just made a huge mistake Randy."

"She tricked me into believing she was you." Randy explained.

"Really, you gonna use the twin thing, you mean to tell me you can't tell us apart? Your five year old child can, but you can't." Latrease snapped.

"I think we need to give them some time alone." Bertha and her family left. Followed by Randys mom and sister.

"Shanice, please tell the truth." Randy begged but she just stood there.

"I believe you Randy. I know my sister. She stole all of my savings too." Latrease stood up and faced her sister.

"I don't understand you. How could you do this to me? After all I've done for you. I'm your sister. I'm the only family you got."

"I don't know." Shanice started crying too.

"I'm sorry, Treasie, I was broke. I didn't know what to do. I got jealous. You were doing so good with your rich family, and I had nothing."

"I accept your apology, Niecy, but you've got to stop doing stuff like this. You are hurting people you love.."

Latrease turned and faced Randy.

"I can't stay married to you."

"Why not?"

"Because my sister will always be my sister. She's gonna always need me and when she comes around I'm not gonna wanna help her; but I won't turn her away. She is my family. We are all we have left."

The room became hotter. Randy felt like he was in a sauna.

"Plus," she added, "I have lied to you over and over. We are not meant to be together, it's clear to me now."

"Latrease, can't you see that everything that has happened to us only brought us closer together. We are meant to be together. You are my soul-mate. Remember, I lied to you for several months. I love you, Latrease Renee Jackson."

Latrease held her head down, a stream of tears flowed from her face.

"We've already been through so much. What's the worst that could happen now. We've already made it past the hard part. There's nothing you can say to me that would make me change the way I feel about you."

"How can you be so sure about that?" she sobbed.

"Because, I love you. And that's what love is about, forgiveness."

"I never had amnesia."

WHITM

Whitmore, Lovely.
It's all coming back to me
now :the secret /
Scenic Woods FICTION
07/13

Made in the USA
Charleston, SC
11 December 2012